The
Daughter

Nathan Driscoll

malcolm down
PUBLISHING

First published 2022 by Malcolm Down Publishing Ltd.
www.malcolmdown.co.uk

25 24 23 22   7 6 5 4 3 2 1

British Library Cataloguing in Publication Data
A catalogue record for this book is available from the British Library.

ISBN 978-1-915046-43-7

Cover design by Angela Selfe

Art direction by Sarah Grace

Map design by Esther Kotecha

Printed in the UK

Contents

Acknowledgements

The initial idea for this story occurred to me fairly quickly but the development, characterisations, plot, description and integration of the historical content took longer. As ever my wife, Jenny, read through several times, gently pointing out where improvements could be made and characters could be developed. My friend and former teaching colleague, Tim Edwards, helped me to understand the components of writing a story, particularly the technique of describing the thinking of a character without writing in the first person. My friend Nigel Smethers was very supportive, encouraging me not to give up in the early stages.

Without the encouragement of my publisher, Malcolm Down, *The Daughter* would never have come to fruition; my sincere thanks to him for helping me persevere. Thanks also to Sarah Grace and Esther Kotecha for their help with the artwork and design. My thanks to Sheila Jacobs for her editorial help and guidance, particularly with what she refers to as 'showing not telling', where the reader is left with unspoken impressions rather than reading what amounts to a news report. With all of these techniques I have an L plate on but I hope that they, at least, are there in some measure.

Curiously enough, after I had finished the second draft, I realised there were echoes of my own family in the story; a kind and submissive mother, an older sister with a deep sense of self-determination and a career-minded father. I am the little brother!

Introduction

The world you are about to enter is very different from the one you live in today. This story is set in Judea, Idumea and Galilee, three regions of the Holy Land at the time of Christ (see the map on page eleven). In Hebrew, Christ was called Yehoshua. Passing references to Christ's ministry, passion and resurrection, and John the Baptist, Herod and Pilate, are historical but Rebekah and other characters here are fictional – they did not exist; I hope by the end of the story you may be able to imagine that they might have.

Rebekah was born into a land where, since the time of Abraham, many tribes and nations had conquered, been conquered, intermingled and intermarried. The Jewish people, who were descended from the tribe of Judah, believed they were God's chosen people. They were exiled more than once, returned and were then occupied by other nations, the most recent being the Romans, who worshipped the sun and other pagan gods. Aramaic and Greek had become common languages, alongside Hebrew. Some Jewish traditions and beliefs had been taken on by the Samarians and the Idumaeans. The Samarians came into being when Solomon's empire was cut in two nearly 1,000 years before Christ and the Idumeans were the traditional enemies of Jacob, Abraham's grandson.

The history of conflict between these various ethnic, cultural and religious groups was deeply embedded in the psyche of the people. When the Romans took over Palestine in 63BC, long memories of occupation stretched all the way back to Alexander the Great in the fourth century BC. King Herod, who ruled from 37BC until soon after Yehoshua was born, inherited deep-seated rifts between the religious rulers known as the Pharisees – who believed they were descended from King David – and Idumeans like King Herod himself, who were said to come from Esau's line. Herod tried to make sure he was in favour with the occupiers, regardless of who held the power in Rome; he was desperate to hang onto his kingdom as far as he could. One of his sons, Herod Antipas, became ruler of Galilee at the time of Christ. He is known for beheading John the Baptist, whose Hebrew name was Yohanan.

In this story, Rebekah is the daughter of Thaddeus, a Pharisee who lives in Jerusalem, the epicentre of Jewish orthodoxy. Many in Jerusalem thought that the Galilean Jews were lesser beings, both spiritually and socially, so the ingrained bitterness from past conflicts and the echoes of warmongering meant that stepping outside of your own comfort zone would be fraught with danger. Rebekah's story proves the point.

Timeline

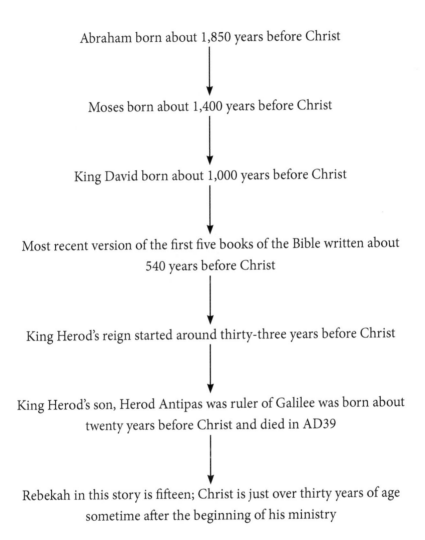

Abraham born about 1,850 years before Christ

Moses born about 1,400 years before Christ

King David born about 1,000 years before Christ

Most recent version of the first five books of the Bible written about 540 years before Christ

King Herod's reign started around thirty-three years before Christ

King Herod's son, Herod Antipas was ruler of Galilee was born about twenty years before Christ and died in AD39

Rebekah in this story is fifteen; Christ is just over thirty years of age sometime after the beginning of his ministry

Glossary of Terms

Hall of Hewn Stones	The meeting place of the Sanhedrin.
Nasi	The president of the Sanhedrin, the highest Jewish court.
Pesahim	The Jewish name for the Passover, when God spared the Israelites in Egypt from his judgement because the Egyptians were worshipping false gods.
Pharisees	A party of priests who believed in the Torah and the oral traditions which followed on from it, as well as the pure line of inheritance from Judah, son of Jacob, through to them.
Sadducees	A party of priests with many similarities to the Pharisees but who believed in the Scriptures alone particularly the first five books of the Old Testament.
Sanhedrin	The Jewish Supreme Court and the governing body of Jewish orthodoxy.
Shavuot	The celebration of when Moses received the Ten Commandments from God on Mount Sinai.
Shohet	A pious Jew who has rabbinical authorisation to kill animals in the way laid out in the Torah.
Torah	The first five books of the Old Testament, including subsequent Jewish rabbinical writings.
Yahweh	A Hebrew word for God.

The Area in the Early First Century

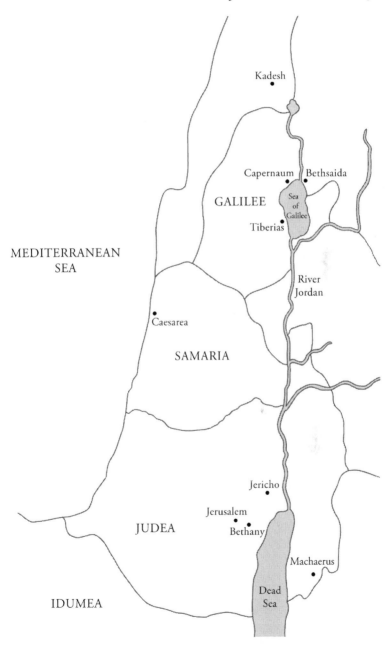

Kadesh

Capernaum Bethsaida

GALILEE Sea of Galilee

Tiberias

MEDITERRANEAN
SEA

River
Jordan

Caesarea

SAMARIA

Jericho

Jerusalem

JUDEA Bethany

Machaerus

IDUMEA Dead
Sea

Prologue

Five teenage friends had come together to celebrate a forthcoming wedding. Decorating each other's hair with a reddish dye made from henna blossoms, they laughed and sang. Eliora, the bride-to-be, had her cheeks reddened with a rouge called *sikra* and each of her friends brought a scent for her which she stroked onto her neck. They all took turns in plaiting each other's hair, undoing it and redoing it in different thicknesses, talking about their mothers' advice as to how to comb it out. They enjoyed some small honey-based sweets and some pomegranate juice and began to talk about the wedding celebration, the guests expected and the decorations on their costumes.

Eliora was in full flow about the colours which her husband would be wearing, when Rebekah asked if she had met her husband-to-be. Curious glances from the others meant there was something unusual about the question.

'Yes', Eliora said, 'but only with his parents and mine present. I expected nothing else; that is our tradition. Our parents choose our husbands for us, don't they?'

The glances now turned towards Rebekah. She knew she had spoken out of turn but sidestepped the disquiet by singing a traditional song to Eliora. As her song finished with the words ' ... she has nothing false about her, she is clean as a doe', Eliora smiled, got up from her seat and hugged the younger girl.

As she returned home, Rebekah saw a pile of stones on the path; she imagined each one to be a member of the family her parents would choose for her. Which one would her husband be, the sharp-edged, small rounded one, or simply the largest? Those feelings of excitement and trepidation faded as she walked on. At least she would not have to think about it for a while.

It would be two years before Rebekah's parents found the family into which she was to be given in marriage. Nevertheless, her mother and father were already deep in discussion about the matter.

'We want a pure Jewish family, of course,' said her mother, Esther, as the afternoon sun on the veranda began to wane. 'But more than that, one that does not have bad blood in it. Our grandchildren must be of good stock. Rabbi Gamaliel's grandfather had a child by a slave – his wife was barren – Rabbi Benjamin's daughter has epilepsy and Rabbi David's son is said to eat forbidden foods. How careful we must be!'

Her husband nodded, sagely.

The discussions continued but gradually another dimension emerged. Rebekah's father, Thaddeus, a Pharisee, had recently been spoken of as a possible member of the Sanhedrin by some influential priests in the Temple. Thaddeus not only wanted her to marry someone directly descended from the tribe of Judah belonging to a priestly family, but also into a family that would improve his standing in the Jewish hierarchy.

One night, as he stared into the sky, Thaddeus felt the weight of a divine impulse as the stars arrowed through the black curtain of the beyond; choosing the right family for Rebekah would help him realise his aspirations.

Chapter One: A Family Problem: Jerusalem, AD27

Eighteen-year-old Malachi had spent the day laughing with his friends but privately worrying about what he might actually have to do to consummate his marriage the next evening. He constantly boasted about his father's teaching of the religious law to young priests, basking in his family's renown. Malachi was expecting absolute obedience from his betrothed – he imagined she would never challenge his authority; after all, that was the way he had been brought up. He himself had often been beaten by Gideon, his father, and he had seen the way his mother was treated. He proudly told his friends, 'When she did not sew enough golden bells on his priestly surplice, my father raised his hand as if to hit her and she shrank away, afraid! My father knows how God wants men to exercise authority in families.' Hiding their own uncertainties, his friends nodded and smiled in appreciation. Rebekah, his fifteen-year-old bride, was expected to conform and if for any reason she didn't, he would make sure she did.

In line with Jewish tradition, Malachi was to visit his bride's home to take her back to his household at a prearranged time; the next day the couple would marry and the celebration would begin after they had enjoyed their first meal together.

The marriage had been arranged between two senior figures in the Sanhedrin, the highest Jewish body: Gideon, a Sadducee, and Thaddeus, a Pharisee. As he approached Thaddeus' house, Malachi started to feel nervous; he wiped his sweaty hands on his robe.

'Are you ready, Malachi?' his father asked him.

'Yes, Father, I am ready,' he replied, knowing exactly how he should act but not how he should feel. He recalled what Gideon had drummed into him – never show your fear. Malachi's father was adept at concealing his own fallibility by making others afraid of him. Malachi himself had learned how to hide his fear by stamping out the whispers of self-doubt and telling himself that he was God's chosen instrument, a future member of the priesthood exercising authority over the people. He wanted to be as driven as his father was.

When they arrived, Thaddeus and his wife, Esther, welcomed Gideon and Malachi into their home. Some of Malachi's friends had arrived outside; the sounds of conversation and anticipation filtered through into the house from the street. Malachi, dressed in his immaculately striped robe and symbolic crown, was invited to go to Rebekah's room to collect her.

Most of the houses in Jerusalem were just one room but Thaddeus' house was on three levels and there were separate rooms upstairs. Thaddeus and Esther had three slave girls who slept in a small courtyard. The roof had a sloping veranda with benches, used in the evenings when it was cool. The lanterns on the roof were a sign that the family was well off. Washing would normally be dried there but for now everything had been put in its place.

Malachi's startled voice cut through everything: 'She is not there! What have you done to my betrothed? She is not there!'

The intensity of disbelief was palpable as Esther rushed into Rebekah's room, coming back shaking her head. A long silence ensued. Gideon looked down at the shorter and slightly more portly Thaddeus in a way that prepared him for the onslaught he was about to face.

Gideon drew breath; he had a habit of speaking as if he were addressing an audience who would hang on his every word but today some of the usual polish was missing; the lines on his face sharpened and his whole body spoke his words: 'You idiot, Thaddeus! You want to bring shame on our household, do you? Where is Rebekah? Have you been asleep for the last week? Has the girl run away? Under our law a child who dishonours her father should be put to death. There must be a price to pay and I have already paid you the dowry – which is now null and void. You have humiliated Malachi in front of his friends; our family is now a victim of your stupidity. What have you got to say for yourself?'

Thaddeus, whose hands were shaking and his face reddening, spat out his reply.

'Don't be absurd, Gideon! Whatever has happened to my daughter, her life cannot be taken from her. It is five years since the Roman authorities permitted us to stone the wife of that Sadducee Zadok for adultery. Look, I am as confused and shaken as you. How do you know she has not been kidnapped?' He narrowed his eyes. 'Come to think of it, perhaps you don't want Malachi to marry a Pharisee's daughter? Something sinister is going on. Have you engineered it without Malachi knowing? I would not put it past you. Is this some kind of ruse to win sympathy in the Sanhedrin? You think you have a chance of becoming the next *Nasi*, do you not? How convenient it is for a Pharisee to let you down!'

Gideon clenched his fists and stepped forward; then he held himself back. He was still close enough for the difference in their height to be used as an advantage.

'You are a clever man, rabbi, but you don't fool me,' he hissed. 'Do you think I would inflict such misery on my eldest son and my family? It is you who are at fault. You are the head of the household and have responsibility for all the members in it. You agreed to the marriage in the first place and I trusted you. If there is no solution tonight, I will take you to our court for bringing shame on our household, our community and our faith. You will have to pay me back much more than the sixty shekels of silver we agreed.' He drew himself up to his full height and spoke in a superior tone. 'Come, Malachi, before we do anything we might regret.'

Thaddeus stood silently by the window as Gideon and Malachi left. The conversation outside turned from excitement to incredulity, and the cacophony faded. One of Malachi's friends put his arm round his shoulder but Malachi pushed him away. As the voices grew distant, Gideon's being the most strident of them, the usual hum of activity returned but Thaddeus' house was silent and cold, even with the mellowing evening sun.

Esther rushed out of the room and Thaddeus sat down with his head in his hands. Eventually, he rose and went to Rebekah's room. The chest was against the wall underneath the window, and there was also a table and a bed. The bed was mounted on feet and Thaddeus knelt down to look underneath. He pushed the cushions aside to get a clear view. He looked behind the drapes over the windows. When he had satisfied himself that Rebekah was not there, he sank to his knees.

'Lord God,' he wailed. 'Why have you let this happen to our righteous household? We have obeyed your precepts and protected your holy Temple. What demon has taken possession of Rebekah, and how has she seen fit to bring her parents into such disrepute? There was no sin in these rooms and yet some serpent has crept in unawares. Rid us of this cursed night and bring us into the light of your glory before the sun comes up, I implore you, O Lord God.'

The kitchen was silent but full of the smells of the kosher meat, bread, mint and cumin which had been prepared for the celebration, all prepared by Jewish hands. The ever-present smell of sewage had been temporarily submerged. Esther was whimpering. She was surrounded by plates of food now to be thrown away or given to the poor. Suddenly she let out a high-pitched shriek, picked up a bowl of delicacies and threw it onto the floor, smashing the vessel into many pieces.

The door opened. 'Rebbetzin Esther,' a young servant said, hesitantly. 'The master wants to see you immediately.'

Esther made an effort to calm herself down before she went upstairs.

Opening the door, she saw Thaddeus sitting with his head bowed. He looked up.

'Esther, answer me truthfully. When did you last see her?'

Esther thought for a moment. 'She went up to her room at midday, telling her friends to go; she said she wanted to spend the remaining few hours in prayer before Malachi came for her at five o'clock. I felt I should leave her to pray.' She put a hand to her mouth. 'Oh, did we not already know that she would not have an easy life with him? He is heartless – whenever I remind you how he beat that servant within an inch of his life for smiling at his sister, you say nothing.'

Thaddeus did not reply. Instead, he stood, and turned his back to her. Esther felt a stab of desperation as she stared at his back and she blurted out the words before she could stop herself.

'Rebekah's marriage was to be the price for your ambition in the Sanhedrin!'

Thaddeus turned, sharply, but his wife continued. 'She is young but not without wisdom!'

'Are you telling me this was your doing? How could you?'

Esther shook her head in disbelief. 'Of course not! I am her mother, not the Tempter, although I was tempted when you decided to make a marriage pact with that family. Power in the Sanhedrin is misery in the home, isn't it?' Her voice had a bitter edge now. 'You chose Malachi because Gideon is his father; yes, a Sadducee aiming for high office. If Rebekah married Malachi, you would be held in greater esteem by the other judges. Your plan has backfired! I give you my word – I went to the market around three o'clock. She must have gone or been kidnapped then.' Sudden tears sprang to her eyes. 'Oh! Has someone taken her? What will happen to us all?'

'Esther! I know you are telling the truth.' Thaddeus put a hand out to her, his face softening. 'What about the servants?' he asked, more gently.

'They don't know anything, not even the Canaanite slave Rebekah was so fond of. She says she heard nothing. The only thing is that the slave's ragged dress and old scarf are missing. Rebekah was quiet for the last two days but nothing more; I thought she was preparing herself for her new life in Rabbi Gideon's family. How wrong I was. Why could I not see it? Why?'

There was a long pause.

'My daughter has brought shame on our house and tarnished the name of the Lord,' said Thaddeus, at last. 'How can a fifteen-year-old girl know what is best for her? I fear the might of the Lord's arm on us all. Next week we have to hear a case in the Sanhedrin – I will barely be able to look at anyone. What will they do to me?'

What will they do to you? What about our daughter? The words were on Esther's lips but she managed to bite them back.

Wearily they retired to bed. After three quarters of an hour the servants of the household would prepare the rooms for the next day but to Esther, suddenly the house no longer felt like a home.

For the next two days there was no news of Rebekah. The family kept silent, with Esther standing as Thaddeus and Eli, Rebekah's ten-year-old brother, ate, for that was the custom. Eli did not speak about the scriptures he had just learned from the Torah, as he would normally do. He had in fact been taught about the regulations to deal with mildew and also about ceremonially clean and unclean food. On a better day he would have recited the verses he had learned off by heart, much to his father's pleasure. Instead, today he just kept his eyes on his plate.

On the third evening Esther broke down weeping and had to leave the room.

Eli looked up at his father. 'Perhaps Rebekah went to find the man who turns water into wine so there would be enough wine for her wedding.'

Thaddeus frowned as he looked at his son. 'So, what do you know about the man who the people say changes water into wine? What does Rebekah know about this?'

'My friends were talking about it; they heard it from one of their servants and I told Rebekah, and I believe she thought one of the slaves might know more about it.' Eli's brow furrowed as he tried to remember what Rebekah had said. 'What did she say... Oh yes! She said, "You had better not talk about that to Mother and Father, Eli." She is *so* bossy.'

Thaddeus had been brought up to believe that God punished disobedience when the law was broken. He wondered what had been going through Rebekah's mind to make her turn away from the life before her. His mind was full of confusion and in the following days he would wake in the early hours wondering what would befall him – would Gideon seek his removal from the Sanhedrin? Would he and Esther have to leave Jerusalem and would their family be destroyed forever? He knew that Esther was angry with him but could not think of a way of appeasing her; she had submitted to his wishes about the marriage but he had to admit – he had always known she was against it.

Chapter Two: The Escape

The day before her wedding, Rebekah's friends had come to celebrate with her; for the moment she had felt happy. She showed them her wedding dress and they went down to the kitchen where the food was being prepared. Singing and praying for a blessed life, Rebekah had been able to forget the reality ahead; she was celebrating the idea of marriage, not the marriage itself. She'd caught a glimpse of everyone else's excitement but when they left, so did her smile. Now the thoughts she had been pushing away with so much effort began to swirl back. *What would life be like if I could choose what I wanted for myself? What does my mother really think, and why will she never tell me? If I ever spoke out my thoughts, my father would chastise me and my mother would have that look of resignation I am so familiar with.* Rebekah had jolted herself out of it and come back to the prospect in front of her.

Gideon had proposed the marriage to Thaddeus and he had gladly accepted. Thaddeus expected Rebekah to take pride in doing her duty to her father as a matter of course; whatever followed would be secondary. Rebekah knew that he had already explained to Eli that the purpose of a woman's life was to submit herself to her husband. When Eli wanted to know why, Thaddeus told him woman had been fashioned by God from one of Adam's ribs.

What Rebekah knew about Malachi had not filled her with hope. Thaddeus had told her about his upbringing – he had been beaten when he could not recite the texts he had been taught from the Torah. Malachi now particularly liked to recite the punishments for immorality and disobedience. He took pride in quoting texts like Leviticus 20:9, 'Anyone who curses their father or mother is to be put to death.' Rebekah had listened to her father impassively as he informed her about Malachi, but she knew her eyes told a different story.

She had also heard from one of her friends that Malachi carried a stick – if any beggars approached him he would hit them, stunning them before poking them in the eye and then laughing. Rebekah could not talk to her father about this because the purpose of the marriage was for his benefit, and to question that would have been to disobey him.

After her friends left, Rebekah had told her mother that she wanted to pray. She went to her room and started off in the usual way: 'Oh Lord God, thank you for finding me a husband who will look after me, who I can have children by, and…' Then she'd stopped praying, and had sat silently, feeling a deep unrest: *Yes, he will look after me through his anger, his demands for obedience and my silence. My children will be moulded into his image: the boys will be driven by anger and the girls pounded into submission. Is this what I want?*

She had thought of running away during the run-up to the wedding, but had not been able to face the prospect of dying of thirst somewhere in the hills outside Jerusalem. But now…

Rebekah did not want to be given in marriage, but women could not exercise such choices. Should she live a short, exciting life rather than a grinding, miserable existence? She knew that even though she was only fifteen she may have lived nearly half of her life already.

Was God telling her that she had a choice? Whether he was or not, she realised that she *did* have one of sorts. She loved her mother and brother and even her father, but her life was not her own. Should she follow the path set out for her by her father, or should she run away, even if she had no idea what might lay ahead? What would become of her?

Rebekah was at a crossroads – and she decided to follow her instincts. In a few crucial minutes she had made up her mind to escape; desperation had overtaken even the unhappiness she would cause by doing such a thing. She prayed again: 'Oh God, please give me the courage to do what my heart is telling me to do; travel with me, even if the journey is short. If I die in the gutter, please comfort me, and go to my mother also when she hears I have gone. I have no plan. I *cannot* love you if I have to follow the wishes of my father. *You* are my Father in heaven and I am walking into the wilderness. Will you, Lord God, leave this holy city and come with me? Even if you do not, I have to go.'

Rebekah had put on her slave's ragged old dress and scarf. She climbed out of her window and disappeared into the busy crowd. The houses were close together and there was too much of a rush for anyone to notice a shrouded wisp of a figure. She had reached the edge of town and merged into a throng of traders, travellers and herdsmen, each with their slaves and asses. The assorted beggars hoping for a morsel made it easier to hide. She hoped she would be carried along by the strength of her will. She began to ask herself: *What journey am I on? I know where I have left but I don't know where I am going; should I even turn back and give myself up?*

For two days she struggled on, becoming weaker and weaker, living on scraps and occasional sips of water offered to her by those along the way. On those occasions she would say 'thank you' without looking up. She pressed on relentlessly, as she knew the Temple police could be looking for her. If they were to find her, her life would be as good as over.

It became harder the further out of Jerusalem she walked, as the crowd became thinner; she kept her head down, for a single glance could be her undoing. Finally, near Jericho, collapsing on the side of the road, she fell asleep. It was not uncommon to see people lying down, unconscious or even dead on the craggy, steep and stony road from Jerusalem to Jericho. Rebekah might be just another corpse in the making and she was left alone. She owned nothing worth stealing.

As she stirred in her half-sleep, Rebekah thought she was playing a game at home with Eli; together they would throw stones to land as near to a chalk mark on a wall as possible. The game faded and she began to shiver. Her body felt hot, cold and suddenly very weak indeed.

Still more dazed than awake, Rebekah now saw the Temple courtyard in her mind. She had been used to going there with her mother every day to buy corn which the servants would later mill. As Esther talked with other women, Rebekah would wait nearby. A young Pharisee called Jacob worked in the Temple keeping the walls and the matting on the roofs in good order. His voice had struck Rebekah as being kind: she had heard him talking to another young man whose father had recently died of fever. Jacob's grandfather, Solomon, also a Pharisee, whose job it was to prepare the ritual sacrifices, sometimes also came into the courtyard.

The voices came more sharply out of her sleep into the present and Rebekah stirred, moving her head to see who it was.

'That girl! I recognise her, Grandfather... from the Temple courtyard.' Another voice: 'Go and see.'

'You are Thaddeus' daughter, aren't you? What are you doing here? What has happened?'

Rebekah looked up through bleary eyes. Was it really Jacob? Kind Jacob? Yes. He was standing there, staring down at her. She found the strength to speak.

'I was to get married but I ran away rather than face being beaten by my husband-to-be, Malachi. I prayed to God and I knew I had to go, even though I had no idea what would happen. You can leave me here if you wish, but I cannot go back; my father will be thrown out of the Sanhedrin and I will become little more than a slave. My mother's life will be destroyed even more than it now is. I do not know what will become of me; being a slave would be a reward.'

'Grandfather...' Jacob explained the situation. Solomon listened to his earnest entreaties, realising that Jacob really wanted to help her. Solomon instantly felt much more protective of his grandson than responsible for Rebekah; he looked towards the girl, and back at his grandson. Maybe accommodating Jacob's concern for Rebekah may help the young man cope with the memories their journey was about to bring back.

After a long pause they came over; Rebekah waited for Solomon to speak.

'You can come with us,' he told her, gruffly, 'as we are visiting Jacob's uncle, in Galilee; if we take you back to Jerusalem on our return, we will be duty-bound to return you to your father. But we will take you for now as the Scriptures say we should "be open-handed" towards the "poor and needy" in our land.'[1] He turned to his grandson. 'Jacob, get some food and water from our ass and let us rest before we travel on. You will have to walk behind us, of course,' he said to Rebekah, 'and what will happen to you once we are there I cannot say; for the moment you can come as a servant.'

Sheer relief flooded Rebekah, and she thanked him, grateful of the food and water they gave her – and the shy smile from Jacob.

After resting for a while, they travelled on, with Rebekah, feeling weak but determined, walking behind them. The following evening, after they had stopped travelling, Rebekah overheard Solomon talking with Jacob. She caught Jacob's voice: 'He is said to have wisdom, courage and miraculous healing powers; everyone he meets has a story to tell. Their heads do not look down, even if they are beggars. He speaks with women and men alike and has angered many for breaking with our traditions.'

The conversation between Solomon and Jacob continued, but Rebekah was distracted. She had heard Solomon say the words '*written on our hearts*';[2] even though Rebekah could not hear everything that was said, the words sounded very different to the way her father used to say them. Her father spoke them in a way that made her fearful; Solomon

1. Deuteronomy 15:11.
2. See Jeremiah 31:33.

spoke them as something to be learned. She wanted to think about just why the words felt so different, but she fell asleep.

They awoke early in the morning and travelled on. Rebekah had never been outside Jerusalem before, for it was only the men who travelled, while the women stayed at home. Having regained some strength she walked silently, seeing the terraces where wheat and barley were grown, the peasants working the soil with hoes and spades, sometimes seeing a plough pulled by two oxen, sometimes dry land and sometimes watered, and then the sudden shock of high crosses dug into the ground; the thought of live crucifixions flashed into her mind. She had heard the sounds of such terrors from her window in Jerusalem but had never actually seen them; the noise of the public haranguing, and shouts of the crowd's pleasure at the spectacle...

Figs, fruit trees, vines and olives: she began to understand where some of the food they ate had come from. Most of the peasants looked as if they lived from hand to mouth; the Temple taxes must have hit them hard. Rebekah saw a group of tax collectors, called publicans, but it was the faces of the peasants that would stick in her mind; they would be left on the edge of hunger as their wheat, oil and firstborn animals were taken away to sustain the Temple and its priests in Jerusalem. It did not escape her that Solomon was one of those priests.

They did not see many Roman soldiers. The tribal conflict throughout Jewish Palestine had been so intense that most of them stayed in Caesarea, and only ventured inland when there was an absolute need to keep order. Even the procurator lived outside Jerusalem in order not to provoke sensibilities about Roman pagan worship. For a short time Rebekah looked at life around her, as she walked behind Solomon, Jacob and their ass; it was a freedom she had never experienced before. She had no idea what would happen to her but for a moment it felt as if she was seeing the world 'out there' as it really was; and hope flickered.

Chapter Three: The Sanhedrin Meeting

A week after Rebekah had run away, Thaddeus went to the Temple. The priests who normally conversed with him seemed to be looking over their shoulders and made some fairly hasty retreats in order to show they were keeping their distance from him.

'Forgive me Thaddeus, but I have to collect a new tunic for Rabbi Levi.'

'Rabbi Joseph is ill so I cannot stop; I have to cover his Temple duties.'

Thaddeus wondered if he was about to be cast out for the sake of Gideon's ambition to become the next *Nasi*, head of the Sanhedrin court. The current *Nasi*, Rabban Shimon ben Gamliel, was ailing and often unable to preside due to illness.

The Sanhedrin court was the highest Jewish court in the land, deciding on matters of religion, pronouncing on individual cases and setting the tone for how the Jewish people should conduct their lives. God had told Moses, 1,400 years before, that he would not be able to shoulder the burden of ruling the Jewish people alone. He was to assemble seventy men of Israel who were known as Elders and take them to the Tent of Meeting. After all that time the elders were still presiding; now they met in the Hall of Hewn Stones, part of the Temple complex, and were known as the Sanhedrin.

The *Nasi* sat in the middle of the semicircle with the members each side of him, sometimes in rows when the full complement was there. The marble hall situated inside the Temple, near to the Holy of Holies, conveyed the sense that the Lord God on High was nearby. The long history of the Ark of the Covenant in which the law was kept included some stark reminders of God's awesome presence; one such event was when a servant of King David assisted a bullock which stumbled when pulling the ark along. The servant accidentally touched the ark and instantly died.[3]

---

3. 2 Samuel 6:6-8.

The Sadducees opposed the Pharisees who, in their view, unnecessarily elaborated on the first five books of Scripture through developing the oral and written law. God had given his 613 principles in Genesis, Exodus, Deuteronomy, Leviticus and Numbers; this meant that there was no need for the Messiah to come, or for other superfluous ideas like resurrection, angels or demons. Why, then, should Gideon compromise his principles by arranging a marriage with a Pharisee's daughter for his son?

The truth of the matter was that Gideon had *wanted* this marriage to take place. While he publicly withdrew from any interest in the politics of Rome, as anything else would be seen as a defilement of his 'purity', he had privately learned a great deal from statesmen like Cicero about political strategy. Simply staying separate from one's opponents would always lead to political atrophy. He knew that he had to win over some of the Pharisees in order to gain enough support to become the next *Nasi*. The marriage would be a means to an end and even if a few hardline Pharisees did not take the bait, he had previously reassured his fellow Sadducees that this would ultimately give them a greater chance of dominance in the Sanhedrin. Again, some were sceptical but most were swayed by his reasoning. However, the plan had now gone astray and Gideon's strategy was about to change.

There were two cases to be heard that day but Gideon now had an additional item to bring to the court's attention. The Sanhedrin members took their seats in the Hall of Hewn Stones. Sixty-eight members were there. Only two were missing due to illness. The *Nasi* was also unwell; Gideon had primed two of his fellow Sadducees to nominate him to take over. No one opposed the proposal.

The first case, one of trespass, involved two moneychangers, Theo and Lantz. Moneychangers operated in the Gentile courts which surrounded the Temple with its various layers of access to priestly courts and up to the Holy of Holies. They exchanged pagan currency for ritually clean coinage, a profitable enterprise. Theo had sent his servant Lek to ask Lantz on the other side of the Temple for some change. Lek had inadvertently climbed up some stairs thinking it might be a shortcut. On the entrance gate to those stairs was a notice which forbade Gentiles to enter. Lek, an Idumaean, could not read. He had found himself in the women's priestly courtyard; he'd panicked and run further, into the male priestly courtyard, where he was arrested by the Temple lictors. The facts were laid out and two witnesses gave testimony as to what they had seen. The matter of Lek's guilt was not in question but the nature of the punishment was.

Rabbi Benyamin, primed by Gideon, was the first to speak.

'If we are to be faithful to God, to the Lord God on High, we must be faithful to his law. The notice clearly says at the entrance to the Beautiful Gate that "anyone who is taken shall be killed and he alone shall be answerable for his death". And again: "The <sc>Lord</sc> said to Moses: Tell your brother Aaron that he shall not enter at any time into the holy place inside the veil, before the mercy seat which is on the ark, or he will die".'[4]

As he said the word 'die' he lifted his arms into the air for effect. He looked around inviting reaction and then continued: 'It is not a question of whether the action was deliberate or not; it is simply about the defilement of a holy place, the most holy place on this earth. There is no doubt that Lek should be crucified.'

Rabbi Mordechai stood up to address the court.

'I am in complete agreement with Rabbi Benyamin about the principle he has laid out but we need to be circumspect: for crucifixion we need the consent of the procurator and we know that his disposition is one of avoiding too much public unrest, regardless of the merits of any particular case. Would it be wiser to wait for when we truly need this remedy? How will Pilate view the trespass of a slave who cannot read,

---

4. Leviticus 16:2, NASB1995.

against the crime of theft? Pilate cares nothing about life or death but a great deal about his own political future. We must be wise and not be too hasty. I recommend that this slave be flogged thirty-nine times and never allowed within the city walls again.'

Although nearly half voted in favour of putting a recommendation to the procurator for the death sentence, the majority needed for such an action was not reached. Rabbi Mordechai's proposal was accepted. Thaddeus was in two minds but he voted for Rabbi Benyamin's harsher proposal, for to do otherwise would have given Gideon even more ammunition against him. Gideon was in favour of the death sentence. Thaddeus thought perhaps Gideon was wondering whether he would have been successful had he addressed the Sanhedrin himself.

The second case, the theft of animals purchased for sacrifice, was less controversial. The two thieves were young Samaritan men about twenty years old. They had nothing to say in their defence and had obviously been beaten by the lictors while in custody. Their fresh-faced confidence had faded away into the shadows of the cell they had been kept in. All sixty-eight members of the Sanhedrin voted for crucifixion. (As it turned out, two days later the procurator agreed, and they were publicly crucified on the Thursday, just before the Sabbath began.)

Thaddeus was about to exit the chamber quietly, when suddenly Gideon got up and spoke.

'I have one further matter to raise,' he said, loudly. 'As you will no doubt be aware, my son, Malachi, was to be married to Rabbi Thaddeus' daughter, Rebekah, a week ago, but through Thaddeus's negligence she vanished on the day before the wedding. She is still betrothed to Malachi and it is our suspicion that she has gone to Galilee perhaps with an accomplice in order to seek out the false Messiah who is reputed to have changed water into wine. I wish the court to authorise my son, Malachi, with the support of the lictors through the Temple tax to seek her out and exercise whatever punishment he feels appropriate.'

There was a deathly silence.

Then Thaddeus stood to his feet. 'I have no objection.'

Gideon asked the court for its approval, which was given unanimously.

Thaddeus left. He could see by Gideon's expression that the Sadducee felt he had saved the day for himself; the members now knew what kind of leader they would have if he were to succeed Rabban Shimon ben Gamliel. After all, Gideon had been brought up to think that if you were seen by the elders to be fulfilling the law, then you would also be seen by God himself in the same light.

On reaching home, Thaddeus ordered Eli to come and see him. He beat Eli with a rod twenty times and told him not to speak of his sister's disappearance to anyone again. Thaddeus placed the rod back in the corner of the room and sat down; perhaps he would survive in the Sanhedrin if he was seen to be in agreement with the arrangement they had made to deal with Rebekah's rebellion. He reassured himself with this and then wondered for a moment what had happened to Rebekah; he felt a pang of concern for her which he could not voice to anyone, not even Esther. Nevertheless, Thaddeus could not think of a scripture which would allow him to put his affection for Rebekah before the law.

Eli went back to his room, whimpering. After a while, he sought out his mother for comfort.

Esther soothed him but made sure he was quiet in case Thaddeus' anger was reignited.

'What has happened to Rebekah?' Eli asked. 'I only *thought* I heard her talking to a slave about the man who changes water into wine. Is it my fault she has run away? Why didn't she tell me she was going to do that? I would have kept her secret; I'm good at that. Now there is no one to tell me stories in the afternoons and play games with me.'

'We must be patient; God will look after her until she comes home, and then you can play games with her again.' A tear rolled down Esther's cheek as she held Eli in her arms. She did not know what to think; as the initial shock had subsided, she had begun to wonder what sort of life Rebekah would have had with Malachi. What a choice: to know Rebekah was being mistreated by Malachi or not knowing whether she was alive or dead, slave or free... Esther was too troubled to pray and felt guilty because of it.

Later, alone, she fell asleep, but woke up in the early hours immediately fearful of everything and unable to sleep again; she was used to accepting her fate, but the pain of her anguish ran as deep as it had when her first two children had died before they were two years old. Esther could still see them suffering from fever following the sudden change in temperature from very hot during the day to freezing at night; the memory of the past had become the present again.

In the morning she called Eli and applied some oil to the marks where he had been beaten.

Chapter Four: Galilee

As Solomon, Jacob and Rebekah left the lower reaches of the Jordan valley, they began to climb away from the fig trees, vines and olives; it was as if the treacherous road between Jerusalem and Jericho was reappearing, as the dusty colours of the rocks and stones enveloped them, broken up by protruding thistles. The brightness of the daylight faded in what seemed to be the blink of an eye, replaced by the coldness of the night. Without asking, Jacob handed Rebekah a blanket; she caught his eye but he turned away.

Near a running stream, they arrived at the farm which belonged to Laban, Jacob's uncle; it was high up near Kadesh in Galilee. He had a flock of sheep and some goats; the kitchen garden looked as if it had once been productive but not any more.

The house was divided into living quarters and a kitchen. There was a large barn for storing fodder and for housing sheep in winter.

As she waited outside, Rebekah heard them all talking indoors. She did not know Laban and it occurred to her that she might be better off running away again. After all, she was a liability, a fugitive from a Pharisee's house in Jerusalem. Why should they take a risk on her?

After an hour or so Jacob came out, and told her to sleep in the barn. He brought her some barley bread, lentils and water. Rebekah said nothing, for the question she kept asking herself could not be answered: *What will become of me?*

In the morning, Rebekah woke and, stepping outside, took in the view. The landscape seemed to have no boundaries, with small clusters of trees in among scrubby fields and rocky outcrops. On the other side of the valley were two or three other houses and barns. Later, she found out what Laban looked like, as he and Solomon came to the barn. Whereas Jacob's face was gentle, Laban's was craggy, weather-beaten and full of suspicion.

In his Galilean dialect, Laban said, 'You may remain with us, provided you observe all our traditions. Your task will be to cultivate the kitchen garden and to prepare food for me after I come back from the hills or after I have been to market.' He paused. 'You must stay here and speak to no one about your past. You must consider yourself a slave and remain near the house at all times. You can collect water from the stream but go no further, and do not speak to other women who are collecting water. If you do not want this, then you must go on your way.'

Rebekah was used to being told what to do. All she could say was 'Yes, thank you for your mercy', as she bowed and covered her head with her servant's scarf.

'Rebekah,' said Solomon, a little more kindly, 'you know that under the law you have disobeyed your parents by running away. It is not for me to judge what was in your heart when you made up your mind to do that. I am a priest in the Temple and when I return, I must inform your parents what has happened to you. It will then be up to them as to what they decide to do.'

Never before in her life had Rebekah been in a place where her future was as uncertain as it was now. The relief she had felt from her escape was fading as the fear of the unknown arose; the fixed agenda of misery was being overtaken by the invisible finger of fate. She had moved from being able to foresee what would happen in the rest of her life to not knowing what would happen in the next hour.

Rebekah wondered why they had decided to wait and see what her parents would do once they found out what had happened. After all, they could have just handed her to some local publicans who were returning to Jerusalem straightaway. Little by little the story began to unfold. It began when one morning Rebekah noticed Jacob sitting alone, gazing out across the boundless vista. He suddenly noticed her.

'You have caught me deep in thought,' he said with a small laugh.

'I will not ask what you were contemplating,' she replied, with a smile.

'I was thinking... thinking of my mother.' And now, he avoided her gaze.

Rebekah plucked up the courage to quietly ask Jacob where his mother was.

'She died when I was born,' he said, without hesitating.

At last, she felt able to ask, 'And your father? What is his name?'

This time he remained silent for a while and then said, 'He was called Joel; that is why we have come.'

He said no more, stood, offered her a small smile, then walked away. Rebekah could not question him further; but she felt her heart begin to feel compassion for this man.

Laban, Solomon and Jacob gathered together in prayer every day and one particular day a few others joined them. From their conversations and their prayers, some of which Rebekah could hear, she was able to work out something of what had happened.

A year before, Joel – Jacob's father – had died. A group of Zealots, who believed that Jews should not fraternise with the Romans, had confronted Joel. They had previously seen him talking with groups of Roman soldiers on several occasions. Following the confrontation, Joel was stabbed and thrown down a steep slope. He landed in a crevasse which was hidden from the road. The Zealots were known for such attacks and several good-natured Jewish farmers had met a similar fate over the previous two years.

Laban had searched the farm and its surrounds with Jacob for more than ten hours before finding Joel. They had heard him groaning quietly as they walked round a steep bend; as they climbed up the slope there he was, his fall broken by a tree. They hauled him back to the house but he died shortly afterwards, having lost too much blood. Laban already knew what had happened from his knowledge of other attacks, and some of the local shepherds confirmed it soon after.

The Zealots believed Palestine belonged to God, not the Romans, and they expected the Jewish people to openly resist them. Once Joel had been murdered, Laban's household was under constant scrutiny. He could not risk hiring anyone who was not Jewish nor eat anything that was not prepared by Jewish hands. Rebekah now understood why he was prepared to take her on as his servant; she had Jewish hands and knew how to prepare ritually clean food. Soon she would be growing the food as well. Laban would make sure it was known that his servant girl, found on the side of the road, was Jewish; the Zealots would turn their attentions to other suspects.

Rebekah soon got into a routine. She would rise early at around 5.30 a.m. and go into the house to prepare breakfast for Solomon, Laban and Jacob. Throughout the day she would collect water from the stream, making several trips, waiting until no one was there. She began to revive the kitchen garden, digging it over with a wooden-handled axe, clearing the soil of stones and nettles. The evening meal was a lentil stew made with cumin and coriander served with cheese made from goats' milk, and sometimes there would be figs as well. She had started to milk the goats and make cheese.

Laban looked after the animals and Jacob helped him. Sometimes they would be out most of the night when dangerous predators such as hyenas, jackals or wolves had been seen in the area. They carried iron bound cudgels to beat them away and knives to kill them if necessary.

Rebekah found herself hoping that Jacob would be all right on such nights – she always felt relieved when she saw him in the morning, safe and well. She wondered if her relief showed on her face at times; she'd given him a drink of water once, and catching his eye, felt herself blush…

After two weeks, Solomon was feeling a pull to return to Jerusalem; the calling he felt to serve the Lord God in the Temple was never far from him. He had spent his life preparing burnt offerings, and strongly believed that he should be there at the time of the appointed feasts. A particular scripture about the Lord requiring 'mercy, not sacrifice' meant a great deal to him[5] – but he also believed that burnt offerings were there to help Yahweh's followers remember their God. In their history, the children of Israel had forgotten their God many times. When they did remember him, they would trust in him, and the Lord God on High would bind up their wounds.

Solomon's own tragic wounds were raw, as he had had to bear the agony of his son's death at the hands of the Zealots. In his inner silence he pleaded for Yahweh's protection for Laban from such murderous thugs. Just as Abraham was asked to sacrifice his son Isaac by the Lord God on High, Solomon also had to bear the pain of sacrifice – only, in his case, the Lord had chosen not to intervene.[6]

Then one day he found himself thinking: *My Joel did not break the law; he conducted himself in line with the whole of the Torah and carried out all his obligations in sincere prayer. There is no instruction in the law to refrain from trading with others, so why, then, was he taken from me? I must accept the will of the Lord although it is almost impossible for me to do so – I am deeply broken.*

Solomon waited and waited before the Lord until he was able to find the will to thank the Lord for something, anything. He spent time reading the psalms of lament but he never wanted to end his times of prayer in despair. He remembered the words of a psalm, 'I will *yet* praise him, my Saviour and my God.'[7] He thanked God that Jacob had come to him after Joel's death, for he knew he might have met the same fate had he stayed on the farm. Solomon thanked the Lord for his provision of Rebekah to work for Laban in the garden, to fetch water and milk the goats, even if it might only be for a short while.

---

5. Hosea 6:6.

6. Genesis 22:2,11-12.

7. Psalm 42:11, author emphasis.

Once he had given thanks for one thing, his heart opened up to thank the Lord for more. A time that began in tears ended with his burden lifting away – at least, while he prayed – until his grief resumed its more or less permanent residence in his soul.

Rising from his time of prayer, Solomon pondered whether Jacob was resolute enough to stay and work on the farm without getting into conflict with the Zealots. He had seen the relief on Laban's face after they had arrived and could anticipate how he would feel if he and Jacob were simply to return and stay in Jerusalem as before. Solomon knew Laban wanted his nephew, Jacob, to stay, but he also knew that Laban would not directly ask for that to happen.

No matter how old they were, children would not challenge or question their parents.

Laban spent a great deal of his own time regretting; regretting that Joel had sold those fleeces to the Roman soldiers, regretting that they thought it a good idea at the time and that it would bring protection, extra money and more opportunities to trade. He felt personally responsible for Joel's death. The Zealots had destroyed his life and he now found himself wondering if they were lying in wait for him behind every twist and turn of the craggy rock outcrops where his lambs would often become trapped.

The Zealots had claimed that Joel had turned his back on God's promise of 'a land flowing with milk and honey',[8] but Laban knew the commandment 'You shall not murder'[9] was of greater significance. He knew that his father's reluctance to openly condemn the Zealots was to ensure that Jacob did not take the law into his own hands. If Jacob were to stay and help on the farm, he would have to be persuaded not to take revenge. That would be difficult because Laban himself wanted to

---

8. Exodus 3:17.

9. Exodus 20:13.

avenge his brother's death but if they were to try anything, the Zealots would cut them down without mercy.

Laban dreamt that they would run the farm as they used to when Joel was alive; they would build walls which would keep all the sheep together at night, including those from the neighbouring farms. They would all work together to make the daily grind easier; he and Jacob might even be able to extend the barn where they would all sleep in the winter, Rebekah at one end and Jacob and Laban near the northern door.

But Laban's mind was racing ahead; he did not really know what would happen and what Jacob was hoping for. Anyway, in the end, his father's wisdom would prevail.

After Joel was murdered, Jacob had fled to Jerusalem to be with his grandfather for fear of his life; he had been with his father on one occasion when Joel had spoken with the Roman soldiers in his broken Greek. After the murder, Jacob found some soldiers to ask if they would mete out justice to those who had murdered his father but they had just laughed and told him to run away. His uncle Laban, when he heard this, made him leave immediately for Solomon in Jerusalem.

Jacob himself felt torn between wanting to be with his grandfather but also wanting to remain on the farm and save his uncle from exhaustion. His grandfather always said everything was in the Lord's hands but Jacob could not see how. He admired his grandfather's faith and could not imagine how he could be so calm in the midst of such turmoil.

Jacob also found himself wanting to make sure that Rebekah had enough warm clothing to stave off the winter cold. He promised himself he would say nothing about her once he had returned to Jerusalem, for he knew that the religious police may well take her, beat her and even kill her. He had heard many priests say that women should be subservient to men; they were not supposed to have minds of their own, but Rebekah definitely did, and for that he admired her.

He often remembered the times they had exchanged a few, brief words. He'd told her about his mother... and his father. He found himself frequently found himself thinking about Rebekah when he was out tending the sheep.

One evening as he thought about her, staring into the fire, he sighed; he had never felt this kind of affection for a woman before, and he genuinely did not know what to do with his feelings.

He remembered glancing into her eyes as she had given him a drink... had she felt the same growing attraction that he did? He shook his head; she was running away from her husband-to-be. Nothing could happen between them anyway...

Rebekah now learned that in another two weeks Jacob would go back to Jerusalem with Solomon. Solomon would visit her parents and she wondered what would then happen. *Will I be punished by my father? At least my mother will know I'm alive, but what will they do to me? Once Gideon and Malachi find out, what will happen to my family?*

When the day came, she watched Solomon and Jacob leaving the farm with mixed emotions – especially when Jacob smiled at her, and her heart leapt. Would she ever see him again? She couldn't think that way.

She began to seriously consider running away two or three days after Solomon and Jacob had left the farm. Would it be better for her mother not to have to bear the humiliation of her enforced return and subsequent punishment? Might she even be compelled to marry Malachi? And then what would her life be – a series of beatings and being made to bear his children?

She found herself thinking: *What is my life? I have chosen my path and I have had four weeks of freedom even though I am a servant; perhaps God has had enough of my rebellion and now I have to take my punishment – my choice is about what sort of punishment that will be. Perhaps I will enjoy my last few days and then run – Laban will feel let down but he will be in even more trouble if the Temple police come for me and he is accused of harbouring a disobedient daughter. If the Zealots hear, they will persecute and maybe even kill him. I have brought this on myself.*

Chapter Five: Yehoshua

Something had caught Solomon's attention. The man who had changed water into wine at Cana was becoming more and more famous. He was teaching in synagogues, healing sick people and calming people who were possessed. People from Jerusalem, Judea, Peraea, Gilead and Galilee were all gathering to hear him, hoping no doubt that he would heal them of their infirmities.

Solomon had decided to travel a short distance to Karn Hattin, near Capernaum alongside the Sea of Galilee. He had heard that this man, called Yehoshua, would be preaching to the crowds there in a day or so.

'Why do you want to hear this man, Grandfather?' Jacob asked.

'I need to know if what he teaches is in accordance with the law, because many are convinced he is another prophet.'

'How will you judge?

After a few minutes, Solomon replied, 'If he rouses my feelings without teaching me more about our Lord God, then I will know he is a fraud. If he contradicts the law, then I will also know that he is a false prophet. If he does neither then I will listen with my heart because the Lord God may be speaking through him. There are some in our tradition who believe there is nothing more to know about God than the law itself. They believe that if you know enough *about* God then you know God. Important as the law is, we want God to touch our souls. We need him to meet us in our grief.'

Jacob was taken aback by his grandfather's directness about the loss of his father; they did not need to say anything further.

Still, as they walked, Jacob wanted to tell his grandfather how much he loved him – but he could not find the words. Their eyes had met without them truly looking at one another.

They came to a flattish mound near the lake and the sound of so many people talking was like hearing a waterfall before coming across it; there was a sense of anticipation in the air. Jacob and Solomon sat down on the grass with about 2,000 people in front of them.

At first it was difficult to pick out Yehoshua, but eventually he stood up from within a small group of men and climbed up a small mound nearby. He began to speak:

'Blessed are the poor in spirit,
for theirs is the kingdom of heaven.
Blessed are those who mourn,
for they will be comforted.
Blessed are the meek,
for they will inherit the earth.
Blessed are those who hunger and thirst for righteousness,
for they will be filled.
Blessed are the merciful,
for they will be shown mercy.
Blessed are the pure in heart,
for they will see God.
Blessed are the peacemakers,
for they will be called children of God.
Blessed are those who are persecuted because of righteousness,
for theirs is the kingdom of heaven …

Do not think that I have come to abolish the Law or the Prophets; I have not come to abolish them but to fulfil them. For truly I tell you, until heaven and earth disappear, not the smallest letter, not the least stroke of a pen, will by any means disappear from the Law until everything is accomplished. Therefore anyone who sets aside one of the least of these commands and teaches others accordingly will be called least in the kingdom of heaven, but whoever practises and teaches these commands will be called great in the kingdom of heaven. For I tell you that unless your righteousness surpasses that of the Pharisees and the teachers of the law, you will certainly not enter the kingdom of heaven.'[10]

The evening after Solomon and Jacob returned to the farm, two of Laban's neighbours came to hear about and discuss Yehoshua's teachings. Solomon was used to remembering Scripture and had been able to absorb Yehoshua's words almost exactly. He was able to repeat them to Laban and his visitors. It did not take long for the visitors to react.

'So this Yehoshua wants to rewrite the law, does he?' said Nathaniel, one of the neighbouring farmers. 'That is proof that he is only after his own glory. How many so-called prophets have we seen trying to rewrite our holy Scriptures? Why do they think they know better than Abraham, Moses and Elijah?'

Edom, another farmer, who enjoyed debating such issues, said, 'But he says he has not come to abolish the Law and the Prophets.'

Nathaniel jumped back in: 'Of course, he had to say that to convince the hearers, but our law is built on the *fear* of God, the *fear* of his wrath and the *might* of his power. The law is about restraint, not kindness, and our God restrains through punishment, not mercy!'

Edom did not answer directly, but asked why so many people were saying that Yehoshua had healed the sick and brought so many demon-possessed people back to their senses. This brought about a pause in the conversation but Laban was the first to comment.

'We Jews have had the privilege of receiving the Law of Moses, so why is our history peppered with so much disobedience? Perhaps the law is not enough? Is that worth thinking about, even if the person saying it is just a common man from Galilee who is trying to seize an opportunity for fame?'

---

10. Matthew 5:3-10,17-20.

Solomon, who had not said anything so far, took advantage of Laban's slightly more open-minded approach. 'Do you recall what the Lord God said to Samuel when he thought Eliab was the right man to take on Goliath the Philistine? It is this: 'But the LORD said to Samuel, "Do not consider his appearance or his height, for I have rejected him. The LORD does not look at the things people look at. People look at the outward appearance, but the LORD looks at the heart."[11]

'We can keep the law with our actions but ignore them in our hearts. There has to be a way where we can combine the commandments with the worship that God requires from us. Think of the life of Job, who thought he was doing everything that God required of him. Why was such havoc wreaked when all that was needed was for Job to acknowledge God's mighty power and incline his heart towards him in a deeper way?'

Nathaniel responded quickly. 'The story of Job was a battle between God and the serpent and the chosen people are here to defend God and his people. Why do you think that David did not kill King Saul, but under the instruction of the Lord God took down the Edomites, Moabites, Ammonites and the Philistines? King Saul wanted to kill David – he was jealous of him – and when David had a chance to kill Saul and put an end to all his murderous plans, he refused because God had anointed Saul and it was not his place to interfere. Saul was chosen by God. But those who were not the chosen people were destroyed. If this Yehoshua is sent from God, why is he not carrying on the line of David by reclaiming this land? I've heard he speaks about loving our enemies! How can loving our enemies be in line with God's purposes?'

'Is that why my father was killed by the Zealots?' Jacob said, plaintively.

Silence followed, then Solomon spoke again. 'We have come to remember Joel and commend him to the Lord,' he said, quietly. 'When David slew the tribes of the Edomites, Moabites, Ammonites and the Philistines, the Lord spoke to him directly. Joel had received no such

11. 1 Samuel 16:7.

instruction and those who took his life have broken the commandment, "You shall not murder."[12] He shut his eyes. 'They had absolutely no direct command from the Lord to kill my son.'

Everyone looked at the floor, absorbing the grief which had appeared like a sudden storm. Jacob himself also looked down, a tear slowly rolling down his cheek.

Laban finally broke the silence and tried to bring the discussion to a close.

'Joel was murdered. Under the law, the appropriate punishment is death but we have no authority to carry out such a judgement; his killers are still free. We must leave it to the Lord; our duty is to look after Jacob. Come, let us go to the table and have something to eat before we return to our homes.'

'Wait a moment Laban, please,' Solomon interrupted, glancing up. 'We must not turn away from our grief too quickly. Jacob should say what he feels before we eat. What do you believe should be done, Jacob?'

Jacob's face flushed. 'The Sanhedrin would be divided over whether the Zealots were guilty of breaking the law, depending on whether they support them or not. The Zealots killed my father for themselves: they used their beliefs to kill him. If I could muster an army of 1,000 I would have enough to beat them down and find the killers who stole my father's life.'

Solomon reached out and put a hand on his grandson's shaking shoulder. His voice was full of gentle authority. 'We understand your anger and share your grief, Jacob, but let us remember what David said to King Saul when he had the chance to kill him. "May the LORD judge between you and me. And may the LORD avenge the wrongs you have done to me, but my hand will not touch you. As the old saying goes, 'From evildoers come evil deeds,' so my hand will not touch you."[13]

12. Exodus 20:13.
13. 1 Samuel 24:12-13.

'David himself said this:

"Do not hand me over to the desire of my foes,
for false witnesses rise up against me,
 spouting malicious accusations.

I remain confident of this:
I will see the goodness of the LORD
in the land of the living.
Wait for the LORD;
 be strong and take heart
 and wait for the LORD."'[14]

Jacob looked at his grandfather, this time directly into his eyes. He rested his head on Solomon's shoulder for a few moments. Then they called Rebekah, waiting at the door, quietly listening to the conversation, to serve them food.

---

14. Psalm 27:12-14.

Chapter Six: A Meal, a Birth and a Journey

Laban had obtained a cut of mutton for the table which had been killed almost instantly by an authorised *shohet* who had cut the sheep's windpipe instantly with a sharp knife. The blood was drained through salting and the forbidden fats and sciatic nerve were also removed. The lamb, seasoned with aneth from fennel seeds, was served together with roasted grain, bread made without yeast, beans and their pods with fig cakes and a glass of kosher wine made from the harvest of a five-year-old vine.

Rebekah could tell from the sounds she could hear that they were all enjoying the food. At the table itself there was a sense of togetherness, of resilience and relief; the Zealots had stolen Joel from them but without knowing, had strengthened the depth of feeling between them.

They began to talk about the oncoming winter, the time when the sheep should come inside the barns. They talked as to how they might combine as neighbours to ward off the wolves at night. Rebekah went back to the barn, and after an hour or so Nathaniel and Edom left to return to their homes.

After a few minutes Solomon began to talk about the return to Jerusalem.

'Jacob, even though Laban needs you here, you must return with me if you are of a mind to seek revenge for your father's death. I understand your feelings, but if you were to try anything, then Laban would be at risk and I would have two sons to grieve for.'

Jacob breathed in slowly. 'Grandfather, I love both you and my uncle Laban, and will not do anything to place either of you in the hands of the Zealots. My father wanted to break away from the hard life of a shepherd and so he tried to become a trader while living in peace with all people.

That was his downfall. He was a peacemaker and so a child of God, just as that Yehoshua said; wicked men have taken him from me but he would not want me to follow in their footsteps. So, although one part of me burns with anger, I know that such anger blots out the memory of my father – a peaceful, decent, kind man. It is a fight that will rage inside me but I must win it for my father's sake; I will not seek revenge.'

Jacob bowed his head. Solomon got up and beckoned Laban. They placed their hands on Jacob's shoulders and Solomon prayed: 'Our Father, God of creation, Architect of heaven and earth, as you saved the chosen people through the parting of the Red Sea, save us, this family; direct us through the wilderness and provide us with an heir in Jacob. Protect his spirit from temptation, comfort his soul in grief and make him strong in your spirit. We praise and worship your name.'

Once darkness fell, the sounds of the night heightened, especially in Galilee; Rebekah had to steel herself to make sure she did not imagine too much. She cast her mind back to being comforted by her mother when she had nightmares. Her pangs of guilt about leaving her mother felt ever more present in the darkness. She had decided not to run off when Solomon and Jacob had gone away. Better to stay and see what would happen... And then there was Jacob – although she had noticed, when she had looked at him earlier, that he had not returned her glance.

Still, she felt some measure of safety. Then the thought came to her that if by some miracle she were allowed to remain on the farm when the sheep came in for the winter, she would at least have some company –and their bleating would dampen the sound of the wolves' howling in the hills. She tried not to think about Solomon's return to Jerusalem, and his telling her parents where she was... and an even worse nightmare than the wolves.

The day after the meal, one of Laban's sheep was ravaged by a predator. Rebekah was told that the sheep would come into the barn at the end of the week, just before Solomon and Jacob travelled back to Jerusalem.

One of the goats had been brought in early as she was nearing the end of her labour. Laban told Rebekah that if the kid was born during the night she was to make sure the sac was broken and that there was not too much mucus in its mouth and nose. She was to make sure the kid was breathing before letting the mother clean it up.

Rebekah had been asleep for about two hours when she began to hear the goat groaning. She watched for an hour or so and began to realise that the goat was really struggling. She tried to feel if the kid was coming out; there was a small gap appearing but with no sign of the front legs. She could not see much anyway as the moonlight was shining on the other side of the barn. She was at a loss; what if the goat died and the kid was lost? Laban would be upset with her for not calling for help, so she went to the house to wake up Jacob and Solomon. Laban was out on the hills keeping guard over the sheep.

She stood at the door and shouted as loudly as she could.

'Come help me! The goat is in labour but the kid is stuck. If we do not help it, they may both die. I cannot hold it on my own and I cannot see in the dark. Help me!'

After a few minutes Jacob emerged, bleary-eyed.

'What is the matter?'

Rebekah explained again, trying to keep the panic from her voice. Eventually, he came out, apparently not wanting to disturb his grandfather. Together they hurried over to the barn with an oil lamp. The goat was in agony but at least Rebekah could see more now. Jacob held the goat from the front while Rebekah tried to see what was happening. There was no sign of the kid's front hooves and it felt as if the side of the kid was pressing against the birth canal.

Rebekah put her hand inside the goat to try to find the front hooves. Jacob seemed to be praying. Rebekah did not know if she was causing more distress by calling for help, but she had to try to save the mother and kid. No one had told Rebekah if this was the right thing to do or not.

Jacob was content to just hold onto the goat's head and shoulders. Rebekah found the feet and pulled them round to the entrance. They just poked out but the head was stretched backwards. She nudged the head round so it was now facing forwards. She put her hand in again so as to push the head down between the front legs and then called to Jacob. He would need to come and pull the feet as she held the mother.

Jacob pulled and pulled and nothing moved. He tried once again and the kid came out with a splash. The mother gave out a loud cry and fell onto her side: the kid lay motionless on the ground.

Jacob held the kid upside down, dangling its back legs, and after a couple of minutes it spluttered and began to breathe. The mother began to clean up the kid.

Rebekah looked at Jacob and this time he did not avoid her glance. Rebekah was exhausted but at that moment had never felt such excitement.

As the dawn broke, Laban returned with a cudgel in his hand. No more sheep had been attacked in the night and Rebekah served him with some bread and honey. Laban drank some of the leftover wine from the celebration. After a few hours' sleep he went out to the fields again with Jacob and they began to bring the sheep back for the winter. It would take two days and Rebekah could see that Laban's relief was palpable; she felt almost joyful. Perhaps it was because the barn was very crowded now, with sheep, goats and feed for the animals and Rebekah was not alone…

Solomon and Laban had decided that Jacob would go back with Solomon to Jerusalem and then return to the farm more or less straightaway for the winter. Laban had hired a young man from a nearby village to help him during the day with the animals, and as the days became shorter, the work seemed to get harder. Solomon and Jacob loaded up their ass and bade farewell to Laban. Rebekah stood at a respectful distance and waved to them. She turned to carry on with her daily work but couldn't stop herself from looking round once or twice.

Laban looked more hopeful than he did when they had arrived. He was a man of few words but Rebekah noticed the expression in his eyes had changed.

'Come on,' he said to her, but not unkindly. 'There's work to be done.'

The weather was grey and as the farm disappeared out of sight it began to rain. For the first hour or so Solomon and Jacob did not speak; a lot was going through their minds. They had been to the place where Joel had died – although Solomon could not bear to look at the exact location.

'Sometimes for a wound to heal it has to be opened up for the air to get to it,' Solomon remarked, eventually. 'We have breathed in Joel's air and remembered him for the man of God he was. May the Lord God look on Joel with mercy and gentleness, just as Joel was kind and gentle with you, Jacob.'

Jacob was quick to reply. 'Grandfather, he brought me up from nothing after Mother died. He was not bitter and always spoke about her love for him and me – for me even before I was born. I can imagine him telling me to use the strength of my anger about his death for good, for the family, for our Jewish brothers and sisters and for all people. He would often say to me that all nations would be blessed by Abraham. I think that is why the Zealots went for him; he had a reputation of being kind to all.' Then he added, quietly, 'I am absolutely sure he would have wanted to help Rebekah if he had seen her by the roadside.'

Solomon glanced at him and nodded in approval. Jacob went on.

'What have we done? Will some say that we should have returned Rebekah to her father's house? Or is she free of them? Is she to be always a slave for disobeying her father… or could she ever marry without his consent?'

Solomon took his time to ponder Jacob's questions. 'When we found her, she was weak and hungry. Our first duty was to help her, and God blessed us by providing a woman who could serve Laban and in doing so, keep the Zealots away. Nevertheless, while she is in our family's care she cannot marry without her father's permission; for us to allow that would be to denigrate our tradition and we would be complicit in her dishonouring her parents. It is my duty to tell her parents where she is and how we came to have her as a servant. We *must* treat her as a servant, but we must treat her well. Her parents will have to decide whether to leave her on the farm or take her back to Jerusalem; it is not in our hands.'

Solomon took a while to see what effect his comments had had on Jacob. Then he said, 'Is that a disappointment to you, Jacob?'

Jacob did not look at him, but he nodded.

'Well… you will be back at the farm soon, Jacob. God will have granted you the gift of ensuring that she is properly looked after, but you must resist the temptation of becoming too close or that may attract unwanted attention from the local priests. I am sorry, but we must maintain our standards according to the law that the Lord has given us; even though she has fled, she is still bound to honour her mother and father when it comes to marriage. If her parents want her to return, she will have to.'

After three days Solomon and Jacob arrived back in Jerusalem. A servant had kept the house intact and prepared food for them on arrival. Solomon went to the Temple, preparing the areas where the burnt offerings were made, and singing the accompanying prayers. He found someone who would be travelling to Galilee in the next few days who could accompany Jacob on the return journey.

Very soon after Jacob departed for the farm, Solomon went to visit Thaddeus and Esther. He explained how they had come across Rebekah at the roadside when Jacob recognised her near Jericho. They had felt duty-bound to help her and took her with them to Laban's farm where she was currently working as a servant. She could remain there if they wanted, but Solomon said that he had told Rebekah that he would need to tell her parents what had happened on his return to Jerusalem; they would have to decide what course of action to follow.

Solomon did not say any more as he wanted them to make up their own minds, even though he hoped they would agree for Rebekah to remain on the farm – not least because that would protect Laban and Jacob from the Zealots.

Chapter Seven: Kidnap

The night after Solomon and Jacob had left for Jerusalem Rebekah could not sleep. It was not just the sheep keeping her awake. She felt that even though she would be protecting Laban from the Temple police by running away, she would be letting Solomon and Jacob down by doing so. She was in two minds about her mother. If she ran away, the first thing her mother might know would be the report of her body being found.

Finally, she fell asleep. And then something happened. A noise, not the animals. Movement. A 'thud' – pain, and darkness.

Her head was pounding. As she regained consciousness, she found herself strapped down on a bumpy cart being pulled by a mule with five or six figures walking alongside. She was gagged and so could not speak. At some point she had been sick, and been left with vomit all over her.

Several hours passed and when the cart stopped, the men took refreshment and food while Rebekah was left tied up. One or two of the men seemed familiar to her but she could not place them. Some water was thrown onto her face and she tried to take the water through her gag before it drained off. Each drip was a precious relief.

It gradually dawned on Rebekah where she had seen these men – in the Temple at Jerusalem. They were the Temple lictors, the 'religious police'. She asked herself how they could have found her. She had not spoken to anyone since arriving at Laban's farm and would always collect water when no other women were at the stream.

Rebekah heard the lictors talking with each other, congratulating themselves on being good detectives. Eli, her little brother, had told his friends that he thought she would look for the man who changed water into wine, and so after the word got around, the lictors came to Galilee. There they met some Zealots who said they had heard there was a new Jewish servant girl at a farm near Kadesh. Laban had wanted to deliberately spread that message around so the Zealots would leave him alone, clearly not realising that he was giving away Rebekah's whereabouts. The lictors went to the farm and they had kidnapped her in the middle of the night. Laban had been sleeping alone at the other end of the barn and the blow knocking Rebekah out had not wakened him – the abductor had wrapped a towel round the piece of wood he used to strike Rebekah on the head with, and the sound was deadened.

After two hours or so Rebekah was untied from the cart and made to sit on the ground. She was then tied to a pole which the men had sunk into the ground, and Malachi emerged from the shadows. His eyes were full of shame, his face glowing with pent-up rage; Rebekah's absconding was a humiliation to him, and that was enough to justify his anger against her. Her refusal to obey her parents would be the smokescreen behind which he could take his revenge.

He approached Rebekah and in the bright light of the fire struck her round the face.

'You have disgraced me and my father's house. I am authorised by the Sanhedrin to administer whatever punishment I choose. You have broken the law of God by dishonouring your parents – your duty is to obey them and the law. You have disobeyed both.'

He ordered one of the lictors to flog her twenty times. She was untied, thrown onto the ground and beaten. Through the pain, Rebekah noticed Malachi smile at the lictors, wanting his legalised violence to be reported back to his father.

Thrown back in the cart, Rebekah could hardly bear the pain of her raw wounds. No longer gagged, she gasped for breath, floating in and out of consciousness, and barely noticed when they arrived at a place where travellers would shelter. A place for the cart and mule was found in an uncovered space. Rebekah's arm was roughly tied to the wheel of the cart and one of the lictors kept guard while Malachi and the other men went into a house to sleep.

Halfway through the following morning Malachi came out, waking Rebekah from her tortured daze. He untied her, and grabbed her by the arm. 'You are my betrothed, and so I will have you and then divorce you.'

Rebekah, still in pain from the beating, hungry and cold, found strength from somewhere. She glared into his eyes, and her voice was strong and cool.

'Malachi, yes you are strong enough to force me if you choose to, but do you want to produce a son who will die as a baby in poverty? I will probably become pregnant and then be abandoned. I will be even more of an outcast than I am now. You could kill me but you might be killing your own son as well. So, divorcing a dead woman with child? Do you want to live with that for the rest of your days? In ten years' time you will still remember my words. And where in the law does it say you are entitled to flog me?'

Malachi was taken aback by the force of her answer. 'You were flogged for dishonouring your parents.' He licked his lips and hesitated. 'All right, I will not touch you. But I have to decide what punishment befits you and report back to the Sanhedrin. My father's position demands it.'

Rebekah found more inner resolve. 'Yes, you have to decide on my punishment, but God will decide on yours. Everything is determined by the Sanhedrin, but the truth is that men like your father and mine battle for power and don't mind who gets in the way. You have learned those ways; you get pleasure from blinding beggars, you are a bully and you use your religion as an excuse to be hateful. You even wanted to use me and then divorce me – where is your heart? Perhaps you should listen to this Yehoshua; he says, "Blessed are the merciful, for they will be shown mercy." I would rather follow him than you. Do what you will; I would rather die than marry you, and you have shown me more clearly than ever that I was right to run away. Spending two weeks as a servant girl is better than thirty years as a downtrodden bearer of your children. If you end up killing me, then tell my mother and my brother that I love them, and tell my father that I forgive him; he could not help himself. I will take heart and wait for the Lord.'

Malachi did not reply immediately. Rebekah knew that he was reflecting on what she had said – but he knew his father would disown him should he be persuaded that kindness was anything other than weakness; he certainly realised that to disobey his father would lead to him ending up in the same position as Rebekah.

'I will decide what your punishment should be for dishonouring our tradition and taking the law into your own hands. I cannot release you, otherwise others might do the same and those pretenders who follow Herod, saying they are proper Jews, will gain ground.' Malachi kicked the ground and the mud sprayed towards Rebekah as he turned and walked back towards the house. He then turned around and kicked the mud harder so it would splatter into Rebekah's face.

'Your brains are in your boots!' she spat at him. He turned round to kick the mud again and she sneered, 'Your father *will* be proud of you.'

Rebekah saw him clinch his fists. But he relaxed them and told the lictor guarding her to tie her arm to the wheel again and to make sure he stayed awake. Eventually Rebekah fell asleep, racked with pain but content that she had finally told Malachi what she thought of him.

Malachi sat down in his room, wondering why he did not feel as satisfied as he had expected to; he drank some sweet wine and turned his mind towards his father and the Sanhedrin. Rebekah was no longer important, he told himself, but he still could not quite escape from the sting of her rejection. He began to rehearse what he might say to his father on returning to Jerusalem.

'She is full of this false prophet's teaching, believing she has a right to discover God's will for her life without giving proper regard to our tradition. I was there at Karn Hattin, next to the Sea of Galilee, when Yehoshua said if anyone looks at a woman lustfully he has already committed adultery with her in his heart. So a woman can be mistreated by a man in the way he looks at her? That is wrong: women are subject to men. In the Scriptures we learn that in war, if you capture a beautiful woman you are entitled to marry her, but if she does not satisfy you, she can be released, but not as a slave.[15] That means she has no choice in the matter. Rebekah has dishonoured our Scriptures and our tradition by thinking she could decide who she marries.'

Malachi had decided that it was too late now; she would never be a submissive wife no matter how much he beat her. Privately he wished his father had chosen someone else, someone who would do what he said; his father had made a mistake but Malachi could never voice his inner confusion. Only Rebekah and her father were to blame.

Malachi could not kill Rebekah without authority from the procurator and did not want to take the risk of trying anything untoward. If he were to contrive an 'accidental' death, the truth might leak out and he could be accused of cowardice for not bringing Rebekah back to Jerusalem. He had to return to Jerusalem with the matter finished and report to the Sanhedrin in a way that would make his father proud of him. His father would find him another wife, this time one who would obey him and bear him sons.

In the small hours a plan came into Malachi's mind. Rebekah should be treated like a captive from an enemy; she was not a proper Jew, in manner, obedience and observance. Malachi had not dishonoured her so he *could* sell her into slavery. She was like an Idumean, someone who purported to be Jewish but had been corrupted by her own wilfulness. The Herodians had ignored the ritual aspects of food preparation and acted immorally in their family relationships. Malachi's father had told him that the Idumean Herod Antipas divorced his wife in order

---

15. Deuteronomy 21:10-14.

to marry Herodias, who was previously the wife of his half-brother – it was against the Jewish law for a man to take his brother's wife. In Malachi's mind, Rebekah's intransigence meant that she was effectively a lawbreaker like Herodias herself. Rebekah would be sold as a slave and if Herod Antipas wished her to be one of his concubines, then so be it. Malachi decided that in the morning they would begin to feed her so she looked better before they made their way to Tiberias where Herod Antipas had built his great city on a graveyard, yet another defilement. This would be a fitting place for Rebekah to spend her remaining days.

Rebekah, still burning with pain, thought Malachi or one of the other lictors would kill her in the morning. So she was surprised when she was given some food, and allowed to sleep in one of the rooms in the house. For the next two days she was kept there and was looked after.

Then, as they made their way to Tiberias she realised with dismay from their conversations that she was to be sold as a slave to Herod Antipas, the tetrarch of Galilee; they had tried to fatten her up to get the best price.

Chapter Eight: A Slave in Herod's Court

Rebekah lay in the cart strapped down while Malachi went to see one of King Herod Antipas' officials. After an hour he returned. Rebekah was untied and handed over. Malachi did not look as she was led away. And so began her new life.

Most of Herod's slaves were Egyptian and from other tribes, and a Jewish slave could be of help if orthodox Jewish priests were to visit and eat with the king. Rebekah would sleep in a small stone cellar with twenty other female slaves. There was a different life going on up above, but her existence was confined to what felt like an underground cavern. Sometimes a few of them would leave the cellar at night and return in the early hours of the morning. They lived on lentils, bread and water; when a banquet, and there were many, was prepared, slaves were allowed some of the uneaten food afterwards.

The other slaves did not look at or talk to Rebekah for the first few weeks, except to ask her name. She wondered what Jacob must have thought on his return when he discovered that she had vanished. Had she run away or had something else happened? Would Laban and Jacob try to find her? Even if they did, what could they do? They did not have the money of kings and emperors; they were shepherds and she was a slave. Now she really was paying the price for her disobedience; at night she silently cried herself to sleep.

By day she ground the corn between two millstones. The flour had to be so fine it could be used for cakes which were flavoured with mint, cumin and cinnamon. Sometimes she would grind the corn coarsely so it could be served with meat. She even learned to make starch and mix it with honey to make jasmine-flavoured sweetmeats. The guards would walk around to make sure everyone was working and if anyone said they were ill they would be beaten. If they collapsed, they would be taken to the dungeons but if they could stand, they were made to work on.

Rebekah could not imagine how she would ever get out of there. Solomon and Jacob's kindness and Laban's need for a Jewish maid, that life back on Laban's farm, they had been the best weeks of her life. Those memories were her only comfort as she thought more and more about her mother. She could see in her mind's eye her unchanging expression as she bore her agony in silence as Thaddeus carried out his religious duties.

Would her father do anything when he found out what Malachi had done? Would her father ever forgive her? Would Eli come to find her when he was older? Would she even still be alive to see him in ten years' time?

Every night all these thoughts would echo inside Rebekah's head until she finally slept. Even when she woke her brain felt it was in a vice, tightening slowly. Time collapsed for Rebekah. She felt like a termite hidden from the sunlight, never stopping to rest and buried in a world of her own making. The darkness, physical and mental, was all-pervading. Her past life was fading away as each week passed; occasionally she began to think of herself as dead. No one spoke of their family; they were all orphans. Slaves who were ill and did not recover quickly would vanish. Rebekah found out that the guards would take them from the dungeons, kill them and bury them in shallow graves in the nearby desert.

When a special banquet was planned, the work increased; from five in the morning to two o'clock the next morning, slaves paused only to drink water and eat quickly. There was tangible fear in the air.

For the celebration of the king's birthday, the king's entourage travelled from Tiberias to the fortress at Machaerus near the Dead Sea. It took two days and the slaves had to walk in convoy. During the journey, Rebekah would occasionally glance up to see if she could recognise any passers-by. Altogether there were about 300 people involved, the royal couple being carried in a litter.

The word was that the king and his wife wanted this to be the best of celebrations. The guards made sure that no one could relax: one slave collapsed and another was beaten for dropping a tray of figs. The day after the celebration, news of what had gone on filtered down to the kitchen. Herodias' daughter danced and the king's eyes had filled with desire. He promised to give her whatever she wanted. Herodias had whispered something in her daughter's ear and an hour later a man's head was brought in on a platter. Herodias had planned it as an act of revenge for this man's condemnation of her marrying the king, her previous husband's half-brother. She had been prepared to use her daughter to arouse the king's desire so he would comply with her murderous wishes.

Rebekah remembered Solomon's repetition of Yehoshua's words:

Blessed are those who mourn,
for they will be comforted. ...
Blessed are those who hunger and thirst for righteousness,
for they will be filled. ...
Blessed are those who are persecuted because of righteousness,
for theirs is the kingdom of heaven.

She comforted herself by saying them silently in her mind. If only those words could change the hearts of the heartless, the intent of the wicked and the cruelty of the powerful, this world would be as lovely as that mother goat cleaning up her kid. The words she had heard Solomon speak to his neighbours were beginning to change Rebekah's own heart. Then she heard some of the slaves talking. The beheaded man was someone called Yohanan. He knew another preacher called Yehoshua and had been claiming that he was the Messiah.

Sometimes Rebekah would plait the hair of the other female slaves and it became known that she was good at it. One of Herodias' maids noticed and Rebekah was asked to go and see her. From then, for two hours a day, Rebekah was taught more about hairdressing by Herodias' maid. Rebekah did not know why this was happening until she discovered that one of the queen's attendants had been cast out because she had signs of leprosy. That attendant was not killed and buried by the guards as they were fearful of getting leprosy themselves. She was simply thrown out of the fortress.

Rebekah was being considered as a possible replacement hairdresser for Herodias. She learned to curl, put ribbons and ornaments in hair and even sew on hair extensions. After a week she was given a trial and Herodias approved.

Now Rebekah had better clothes and better food and began to see what was going on up above. The rooms were spacious, decorated and furnished, sometimes with sculpted animals to adorn the headrests on the beds; she did not allow herself to think too much about the difference between upstairs and the dark, dank cellar she slept in. The world above was a temporary sojourn; the cellar was 'home'.

One day Rebekah was waiting to attend to Herodias' hair in preparation for a visit by the queen to a Roman centurion. The custom was for her to wait in an adjoining room before being called. It sounded as if Herod had been drinking for several hours.

'Why did my father leave me the dregs of his kingdom?' Herod Antipas complained. 'None of this would have happened if he had left me Judea, Idumaea, Samaria and Bashan rather than the backwater of Galilee. Archelaus received the lion's share because he is the eldest, but I have my father's name. I want the whole kingdom now. How long must I wait?'

Herodias was clearly used to the king when he had been drinking, and her tone was soothing.

'When you are sober you will see more clearly. Be patient and gather up more swords, knives and javelins, as you have been doing. When you have enough, then you will need to recruit soldiers from the common people and gather up chariots and horses, but for now you must wait. You cannot win the battle yet. If the Romans find out about your store of arms in the basement, tell them they are there in case we are attacked by the Arabs from the north. I hope they believe you. In the meantime, Salome and I will keep the Roman centurions and the procurator happy; you will need to time your assault to give yourself the best chance of capturing more land. You cannot take the Romans on so you need to convince them that your kingdom's extension is in their interests. They have to believe that your extended rule will assist them in their occupation. I am visiting Accasius today; he always appreciates my conversation. I cannot talk now; my hairdresser is waiting.'

'Y-e-s… he will enjoy conversing with you; I wonder what you will discuss?'

Rebekah was summoned into the room. She came in, eyes lowered, asking, 'How would the queen like her hair today?'

'I want it tied up with a broach but layered in a way that will become easily free,' Herodias answered, but in an afterthought added this warning: 'You are good at preparing my hair, but there are plenty of others who can do just the same. Be very careful how you talk downstairs.'

Rebekah knew that at night many of the guards at Machaerus were consorting with the maids. Then, one day, a king's officer called Esau ordered Rebekah to come to his room that evening. She knew that if she refused, she would probably be accused of theft and chained in the dungeons, for women had no say in such matters. She would most likely be abused by the dungeon keepers and then thrown out. She would be too unwell to attend to Herodias' hair. The fortress was too heavily guarded for her to run away.

Rebekah found herself retching at the thought of what lay ahead. She prayed to the Lord God for mercy. She wished she could ask Solomon what to do but she was trapped and Jerusalem was two days walk away; an impossibility. In her despair, an idea occurred to her. She went to the kitchen when no one noticed, mixed up some very small rotten meat scraps with a little porridge and some pods and carried it back to her room. The smell was intense.

Rebekah duly arrived at Esau's room and as she began to undress, he began to sniff the air.

'What is that?' he asked.

'I have a disease,' she replied calmly, continuing to disrobe.

'What! Is it contagious?'

'I don't know.' Rebekah stopped and waited while he hesitated.

'Show me' he said.

He looked and instantly recoiled, sitting down with his head bowed. But then he started to remove his clothing. Rebekah felt sick. Her plan had failed.

Then suddenly he turned to her and said, 'You may go. Tell the slave Masika to come here immediately.'

Rebekah went to find Masika. She knew this girl normally went to Esau, and she also knew that Masika had given her some very icy looks since she'd found out that Esau wanted Rebekah. Rebekah wondered if Masika had come to view her as a threat.

'He wants you, not me,' Rebekah repeated, and at this Masika's untrusting face brightened and she prepared herself to go to him. Rebekah returned to her room and fell to the floor thanking God for his mercy. She even thanked Solomon.

Rebekah decided that she would have to walk around with that faint smell at times, especially when the royal guards were around. Together with the rumours which would inevitably circulate, Rebekah already felt safer. She was sorry for the maids who had no choice; she would have told them her ploy but then it would have been discovered. She wondered if Herodias would question her... but she always made sure she was clean when she attended to her hair.

Chapter Nine: A Familiar Voice

Esther had lost two of her children even before they were two years old and now she only had Rebekah and Eli left. Rebekah had run away and Eli was bereft without his sister. When she thought about Rebekah, which she did almost all the time, she wavered between anger and sympathy; Rebekah had brought shame on the family but she had also run away from a life which would have been far worse than Esther's own. Thaddeus was a traditional Pharisee but he did not have that cold, cruel streak which Gideon and Malachi relished. Her life was harsh but not unbearable; Rebekah would have suffered terribly with Malachi.

Misery had wound itself into Esther's face as each deep line travelled out from her soul for those around to see.

As ever, the tension in the household increased as the next Sanhedrin meeting approached. Esther could not bear the thought of Rebekah being brought back to Jerusalem and then being forced to marry Malachi, because if that were to happen, she would be repeatedly beaten and abused. Thaddeus had finally decided that he should ask the Sanhedrin to allow Rebekah to remain as a slave on Laban's farm as punishment for her disobedience. He thought the Sanhedrin would be satisfied because he was refusing to have Rebekah back in his household; it would show that he strongly disapproved of her behaviour.

The whole of the Sanhedrin was assembled for the meeting. The ailing *Nasi*, Rabban Shimon ben Gamliel, was in the presidential chair, and the Temple court looked especially busy on that day.

There were two items on the agenda:

1. Malachi's report, to be presented by his father, Gideon.
2. Action to be taken concerning Yehoshua, the false prophet.

After the *Nasi* had prayed to open the meeting, Gideon rose to speak.

'I wish to remind you that it was decided, following Rabbi Thaddeus' negligence in controlling his daughter, Rebekah, that my son, Malachi, the betrothed, would be sent with a group of Temple lictors to seek her out and exercise an appropriate punishment. As Malachi is not yet authorised to speak to the Sanhedrin, I will relay his actions to you.

'Rebekah was discovered to be sleeping in a hill farmer's barn near Kadesh. A group of Zealots informed Malachi that a new servant girl had been taken on by the farmer. Rebekah was taken to an inn and questioned about her behaviour. She was unrepentant about dishonouring her family, and the marriage traditions handed down to us through many generations, believing that she herself could determine who she married. In this she was disobeying the fourth commandment. For this breach she was given a flogging of twenty lashes by a lictor.'

Thaddeus kept his head bowed throughout but once or twice he looked up at Gideon. Gideon's eyes were deep, resentful and full of purpose. He continued: 'I like to think, Thaddeus, that had you been in a position to administer the flogging, you would have done so yourself. What became apparent to Malachi and the lictors was that Rebekah had been brainwashed by the teachings of the false prophet, Yehoshua. Essentially he teaches that what he calls mercy is a justification for ignoring our traditions, the Sabbath, and the punishments laid down in the Law of Moses. How can the law be upheld if there is no fear of punishment? You know the Scriptures but let me remind you: "The fear of the <sc>Lord</sc> is the beginning of wisdom".[16] "Blows and wounds scrub away evil, and beatings purge the inmost being."[17]

'Malachi became convinced that Rebekah was not suitable to bear his children. Under the strictest provisions of the law, it would have been legitimate to punish Rebekah with death by stoning as she had

---

16. Psalm 111:10.
17. Proverbs 20:30.

effectively made herself an adulteress by seeking a life outside of the pure practice of the Jewish faith. She had run away to Galilee, to where the tetrarch, Herod Antipas, chooses to call himself a Jew but ignores the ritual cleanliness of food preparation and many other aspects of the Torah. Out of mercy towards Thaddeus' family, Malachi did not choose to ask the Roman procurator for the death sentence but instead confirmed Rebekah's adulterous state by selling her to Herod Antipas as a slave.

'The law says, "Your male and female slaves are to come from the nations around you; from them you may buy slaves."[18] In rejecting the requirements of the Torah, Rebekah has made herself as if she were a member of a foreign tribe; accordingly, she was sold to a tribe that is not of King David's line.

'In consequence of this, I wish to announce that Malachi is no longer formally betrothed to her. Do you have anything to say, Rabbi Thaddeus?'

Thaddeus rose to his feet, knowing that his original request for Rebekah to stay on the farm would now have to be abandoned.

'I want to thank Malachi and Gideon for treating my daughter, Rebekah, with mercy. May God himself have mercy on her and on our family which has had to bear the shame of this tragedy. I want to assure all of you that I remain faithful to the Sanhedrin as God's instrument of justice and that I hope that one day soon, true observance of the law will prevail across this land.'

The *Nasi* announced that the matter was now dealt with and closed with a verse from the Torah: 'All these curses will come on you. They will pursue you and overtake you until you are destroyed, because you did not obey the LORD your God and observe the commands and decrees he gave you.'[19]

---

18. Leviticus 25:44.
19. Deuteronomy 28:45.

Rabbi Nathaniel then opened the discussion on what action should be taken about the false prophet, Yehoshua.

'We have already heard about the insidious effect that this Yehoshua has had on Rabbi Thaddeus' daughter, but his reputation is spreading across all of Galilee and the neighbouring lands. Word has it that he is claiming to be the anointed one, "one who will be ruler over Israel, whose origins are from old, from ancient times".[20] How can this be? He is an imposter – and why? Because God has said he will speak through the elders; yes, *this* body of men, whom the Lord on High has chosen to speak through to his people from the time of our forefathers. When the Messiah comes, he will come into this land as a child of one of *our* families, a family God will choose from *us*. For all we know he may already be with us. Whether or not Yehoshua carries out miracles is not important, because Satan can do miracles as well.

'This Yehoshua is undermining the true nature of God's voice on this earth. He must be stopped; the only question is how and when. We have to find a way of getting the procurator to agree the death sentence, and the sentence for blasphemy is death, for the scripture says that anyone "who blasphemes the Name of the Lord must be put to death".[21] The entire assembly must stone him.'

Rabbi Daniel intervened: 'Yes, Rabbi Nathaniel, but Pilate will not let us carry out the death sentence without his authority and could refuse us permission. What would we then do?'

Rabban Shimon ben Gamliel, raised his hand and Rabbi Daniel broke off allowing the *Nasi* to speak.

'We will first have to capture this Yehoshua and then build a case against him. We must find a way of convincing Pilate that he is a traitor and an enemy of Rome, even though he is first and foremost an enemy of God. He is disloyal to Augustus, he is disloyal to the Lord God on

---

20. Micah 5:2.
21. Leviticus 24:16, NLT.

High, he is disloyal to the Sanhedrin, and so he is guilty of treason. This is the message we must quickly spread across Israel, and influence rabbis to call out this blasphemy in our synagogues. We will have to work out how to capture him. We must deal with this now, before it gets out of hand. What suggestions do you have?'

Rabbi Joshua was the first to raise his hand. 'Let us pay one of the Temple guards to feign interest in the teachings of this Yehoshua and so get close to one of his followers. We will instruct him to find a follower who is either poor, greedy, or both, and befriend him. Then at the right moment an offer of thirty pieces of silver will be made for him to disclose the whereabouts of Yehoshua at the appropriate time. We will then approach Pilate and say the man must be arrested, otherwise there will be a riot.'

After some discussion as to whether this would work, the *Nasi* put the motion to the vote. Sixty-one were in favour of the proposal while nine did not vote. Thaddeus voted for the motion; to do anything else would have put his family at risk, including Rebekah.

Gideon rose to his feet and the *Nasi* signalled for him to speak.

'We Sadducees and Pharisees have our differences, but today we face a common threat to our faith and tradition as a whole. We must not shrink from the task. I agree we need to convince the common people that this man is a blasphemer. We do need a strategy to capture him, but we also on this occasion need to cross into enemy territory. Despite what I have said on past occasions about Herod Antipas and his purported imitation of the Torah, this Yehoshua is very popular in Galilee, and I believe we should send a delegation to Herod Antipas to work with him in pursuing and putting this false prophet to death. In the interest of unity, let a few of us go to the tetrarch and seek his help. Herod does not like those who question his authority, as the man who lived on locusts and wild honey, Yohanan, found out to his cost.'

There was a general mood of assent to this proposal and Gideon finished, 'I would like to go with four others. Rabbi Thaddeus, can we put our differences aside and work together to eradicate this poison from within our midst? Will you join me?'

Having satisfied the requirements of the law, Gideon now obviously wanted to present himself as magnanimous; suddenly being generous would make him less predictable and keep his supporters on their toes. Thaddeus knew that for Gideon, God punished first and then showed mercy to whoever he chose and that is how Gideon himself wanted to be seen by his fellow priests.

Thaddeus thought ahead to what Esther would say when he told her that he must work so closely with the man whose son had caused Rebekah such suffering. But he realised he had no choice if he wanted to remain as accepted in any measure, so he steeled himself and replied, 'I will come with you, for what joins us together is greater than that which separates us. Remember your namesake, Gideon. The Lord started with 32,000 men, many of whom were afraid. He reduced the number to 300 fighting men and won the battle against the Midianites. We must do the same.'

When Thaddeus arrived home, he told Esther everything that had happened. She flinched when she heard that Malachi had found Rebekah, and grimaced on hearing that Thaddeus had been pressurised to consent to Rebekah's flogging. Thaddeus told her of the planned visit with Gideon to Herod Antipas.

'You must do what you must do,' she told him.

Esther went to her room and prayed for Rebekah. Suddenly, she decided to no longer pray silently – perhaps Rebekah's courage had rubbed off on her. She did not deliberately want Thaddeus to overhear, but wanted to hear herself pray: 'Oh God in heaven, I praise your name that Rebekah is still alive, even after being in Malachi's hands; it is a miracle she has survived. If you can grant it, may I see her once again? Keep her safe and free from violation, I pray. May she have enough to eat, and a warm place to sleep. May her heart be consoled with your comforting presence. Thank you, God, that she is still walking on this earth you have created! Please God, may she know that I forgive her, despite everything.'

Thaddeus overheard part of Esther's prayer and began to question himself privately. Even though he could not hear all her words, her tone was fearless. Were his ambitions in the Sanhedrin worth all the distress? Was he truly acting righteously in the eyes of God? Would he have flogged Rebekah twenty times? Was Gideon really speaking with the Lord's authority?

In spite of all this, he could not see an immediate way out of his predicament. He thought for a while, and then went about preparing for his visit with Gideon and the other three from the Sanhedrin to Herod Antipas.

Herod Antipas had decided to go to Jerusalem from Machaerus a few weeks ahead of the Passover and took Herodias with him. About twenty of the guards and slaves, including Rebekah, accompanied them. After a few days in Jerusalem, a delegation from the Sanhedrin came to discuss how they might jointly deal with the threat of Yehoshua. Herodias knew that Rebekah was Jewish, so she was asked to ensure that the food was prepared according to the customs which the Pharisees and the Sadducees would be content with.

A banquet was prepared but with less excess than usual. Herod wanted to impress his guests with how restrained he was. There were no women present, except those who would serve. The menu consisted of roasted ox and antelope; Herod ensured that the draining of the blood was carried out by an authorised *shohet*. The meat was served with radishes and cucumbers and seasoned lentils along with bread. Dark kosher wine with figs and grapes accompanied the meal.

Five members of the Sanhedrin arrived and after a short period, they sat down to eat with Herod Antipas along with two of Herod's high-ranking officers. Rebekah was in an adjacent room checking the food before it was served by the other slaves. As the food was brought in and served and plates refilled, she was able to hear snatches of their conversation.

'This Yehoshua is a much greater threat than Yohanan ... many more are coming from all parts of ... healing first and then providing bread.'

'A threat to the social order in Galilee and Judea ... cannot be ...'

'Unless he is silenced soon, Pilate will come down on us all ... is turning law-abiding Jews into rebels ...'

'Can we, on this occasion, work together to capture him and stop this uprising?'

And so it went on, but as the meal was coming to a close Rebekah heard a very familiar voice: 'Perhaps we should, together with your officials, visit the procurator to warn him of the impending trouble which will occur if this man comes to Jerusalem at the time of the Passover...'

Rebekah nearly collapsed in shock; it was her father's voice. Her first instinct was to rush in and fall at his feet, but she held herself in check. If she made herself known, it could cause them both great trouble. She thought her father would be humiliated and could be removed from the Sanhedrin. At the very least, Rebekah would be sent back to do the most back-breaking work or sold to a distant, foreign tribe.

She waited, and carried on with her duties, and when the visitors left, made sure that she was not seen by any of them. It was a strange kind of 'mirage', hearing her father's disembodied voice; was this the nearest she would ever get to her family again?

When Thaddeus returned home, Esther came running. 'Well, did you see her?'

Thaddeus shook his head and retired without saying a word.

Chapter Ten: Yehoshua's Fate

As a child, Rebekah had been taught about the Passover by her father. In ancient times, around 1,300 years before, God had decided to judge the Egyptians for their worship of false gods. He passed over the houses where the Jews, slaves of Egypt, had dripped the blood of sacrificial lambs onto doorframes, and they were spared. All other firstborn males and animals were slain, and the Jews were set free from Egyptian slavery. It was the most important annual festival in the Jewish calendar, called the Pesahim.

King Herod Antipas had stayed in Jerusalem to show his respects to the Jewish authorities over the holy week. He was not the only person who came to celebrate God's mercy to the Israelites. After the Babylonian invasion, 600 years before, many Jewish people had been scattered abroad. From these far places, pilgrims still came to Jerusalem for the Pesahim. For those travelling by sea, they would land at Joppa and walk for two or three days to Jerusalem. The streets were full of men singing psalms off by heart. Up to five times the number of people who normally lived in Jerusalem would crowd the city streets.

They came to Jerusalem because men were duty-bound to present themselves to God to mark the anniversary of the journey out of Egypt to Canaan, the Promised Land. The centre of the Jewish faith was the Temple in Jerusalem. Each man had to bring an unblemished lamb for sacrifice and because there were so many of them, each with a lamb, the drained blood would flow down the gutters into the river Kidron. All the entrails and the fat were burnt and the stench stayed in the air for the whole week; it was a smell Rebekah was familiar with from her youngest days.

However, the real reason Herod Antipas had come to Jerusalem was to buy more swords and knives for his armoury. He thought the Roman authorities would be preoccupied with the crowds and so he would seal his purchases without being noticed; the deliveries would be made later on. He was not expecting to be drawn into a battle between the Sanhedrin and the Roman procurator, Pontius Pilate.

Herodias had called Rebekah to her chamber to dress her hair, and Herod came in and sat down nearby. She had not asked him until now about the delegation from the Sanhedrin as she thought it was of little importance. 'What did they want?' she said, casually.

Herod, who always took a moment to try to work out what was behind her questions, replied, 'It was to rid them of yet another Yohanan; this Yehoshua is apparently healing people and doing miracles. They say he has fed 5,000 people with a few loaves and some fish. They think he is a threat to their way of life and most of all, he claims divine authority. He criticises them in the same way Yohanan spoke against me. I agreed to visit Pilate with them to warn him; we went yesterday but Pilate was unconcerned.'

Herodias laughed. 'Perhaps we ought to employ this Yehoshua as a cook? At least he has not condemned our marriage, otherwise we would have his head as well. Two heads? What a collection!'

Herod got up and walked across the stone floor to a table where there were some olives and figs.

'He lost his head because you wanted to silence him for saying we are illegally married,' he said, his mouth full. 'I was drunk and I made you a promise, and for that reason alone he lost his head. You had inflamed me with your Salome's seductive dancing. I actually found him quite intriguing; who cares what these wild men say? They are not the Roman occupiers who I have to contend with. They are not the ones who will prevent me from taking back from my brothers what is rightfully mine. We have to keep on friendly terms with Pilate and when the time comes to retake our lands, as you say, we will have to persuade him it is in his interests.'

A few hours later, a guard came in to tell Herod Antipas that Pilate had just sent Yehoshua to him because he was a Galilean and therefore Herod's responsibility. Along with the Roman soldiers who brought him were also a whole crowd of priests and teachers of the law, shouting questions at Yehoshua.

Herod knew that Pilate was trying to shift the responsibility for dealing with this uncomfortable situation onto him. He would have gladly obliged in order to stay in Pilate's favour, but it was not as simple as that; Herod would need the common people on his side when it came to expanding his domain – it was not worth risking their support. He had already decided to return Yehoshua to Pilate after questioning him. The whole household could hear what then happened during the interrogation, as Yehoshua was dragged in with a crowd of those who accused him. Rebekah looked on from an upper window. The throng had worked themselves up into a frenzy of accusations.

'You said a woman caught in adultery could go free; where does the law say that?'

'You do not deny healing someone on the Sabbath? Why do you break God's commandment without shame?'

'You consort with women and make them your disciples, you eat with sinners and criticise our Temple tax system, denying our traditions; you have no loyalty to the Lord God on High. Do you repent?'

'You have committed the ultimate blasphemy by saying you are the Son of God; what is the punishment in the law for that? It is death.'

They began to shout, 'Prophesy, do a miracle, why don't you repent? You are a blasphemer!'

Then Herod asked Yehoshua where he received his authority from, how he knew more than the scribes and the Pharisees, why Pilate had no time for him and why he had been sent to him when he had better things to do with his time.

'Perhaps I might be convinced if you could make the river Jordan run dry or turn a man into stone. You say you can do anything – well go on, and make fools of us all.'

In all of this, Yehoshua said nothing. Herod Antipas and his soldiers began to say he was mad, an entertainer and a demon-gatherer. Herod said to the soldiers to dress him in purple and return him to Pilate.

'Before you go,' he said, 'can you sing us a song?'

Rebekah saw Yehoshua's face clearly just the once – and to her surprise, he did not look angry or frightened: he looked brave. After he had been taken away she cried for him, remembering his words: 'Blessed are those who hunger and thirst for righteousness, for they will be filled.'

She was glad he did not answer their questions, because she knew they were only trying to ridicule him so they could throw still more insults at him. They were so cruel, but what really disturbed her was the enjoyment they derived from their cruelty. It reminded her of Malachi.

Herod Antipas' guards escorted Yehoshua back to Pilate. Later in the evening Herod invited Pilate for drinks, as he wanted to reassure Pilate that he did not sympathise with Yehoshua.

As Herod Antipas and his entourage travelled back to the fort at Machaerus when Pehasim was over, it became apparent what had happened to Yehoshua. Rebekah heard the guards talking.

'Those Jewish priests wanted him dead, even though Pilate could not find him guilty.'

'Pilate just wanted rid of it; he released a thief instead, just to keep them quiet.'

'Oh well, that's the end of him, just like Yohanan. His followers will go into hiding until the next Saviour springs up from the hills!'

Rebekah prayed silently as she walked: 'Lord God, I want to hunger and thirst after righteousness. I want to be shown mercy, but I cannot find mercy for cruel, wicked people who kill others. Yehoshua is dead, but his words are not.' And as she prayed, she remembered some scriptures that her mother had read out loud to her when she was a child:

My God, my God, why have you forsaken me?
Why are you so far from saving me,
so far from my cries of anguish?
My God, I cry out by day, but you do not answer,
by night, but I find no rest.

Yet you are enthroned as the Holy One;
you are the one Israel praises.
In you our ancestors put their trust;
they trusted and you delivered them.
To you they cried out and were saved;
in you they trusted and were not put to shame.

But I am a worm and not a man,
scorned by everyone, despised by the people.
All who see me mock me;
they hurl insults, shaking their heads.
'He trusts in the LORD,' they say,
'let the LORD rescue him.
Let him deliver him,
since he delights in him.'

Yet you brought me out of the womb;
you made me trust in you, even at my mother's breast.
From birth I was cast on you;
from my mother's womb you have been my God.

Do not be far from me,
for trouble is near
and there is no one to help.[22]

---

22. Psalm 22:1-11.

And then it struck Rebekah that God must have already known that Yehoshua would suffer such humiliation. She felt strangely comforted and wondered why her mother had chosen to read her those scriptures. Did she somehow know what might happen to Rebekah? Perhaps what was happening to Rebekah had already happened to her? Perhaps she silently suffered in the same way that Yehoshua did when he was belittled by Herod and the Pharisees? Now Rebekah could see her face with its loving kindness towards her, doing her best to shield her from her father's anger. But as she thought of her mother's kind eyes, she could now also see something she had previously noticed but not fully understood – overwhelming sadness.

Chapter Eleven: A Political Release

The slave girl Masika had regarded Rebekah with suspicion when she became one of Herodias' hairdressers. Anyone who had access to Herodias had the potential to make life difficult for other slaves. But there seemed to be almost a respect between them, since Rebekah had told her that Esau preferred her; and Masika had decided to pass on information to Rebekah in the hope that she would not speak badly of her, should Herodias ask the Jewish girl about the other slaves.

Shortly after Herod had returned to the fort at Machaerus, Masika whispered something in Rebekah's ear, something which Esau, the officer Masika was obliged to sleep with, had told her. When the Jewish leaders had previously visited to ask for Herod's cooperation in persuading Pilate to stop Yehoshua gaining favour with the people, Gideon had taken Herod aside as they were leaving and told him to be careful of Rebekah: 'You have a slave called Rebekah; she is the disobedient daughter of Thaddeus, who is the short, plump rabbi who was sitting to your left in our meeting. He spoke about us visiting Pilate together to warn him of Yehoshua. Watch out for her; she is an untamed rebel. She ran away when she was already betrothed to the son of another family.'

Taking care not to mention that it was his own son who Rebekah had been betrothed to, Gideon had clearly thought it would be of benefit to him to ask Herod to return the favour when it was needed; little did he know that his wish to seek revenge on Rebekah would in fact save her life. Herod was more interested in his own political standing than in simply keeping his household in order. So, for him to arrange for a Jewish slave to meet an untimely end could cause an unwanted backlash from orthodox Jews who played to his tune when it suited them, but in reality despised him.

As the festival of Shavuot approached, Herod made plans to visit Jerusalem again. He wanted to be seen as honouring the Jewish festivals as well as tie up some loose ends on the arms deals he had previously made with various traders. The queen feigned illness to avoid going, even though Herod had thought it was a ploy. Once Herod had left, a series of male visitors would come to see Herodias in the afternoons and Rebekah was as busy as ever doing her hair, always in a way in which it could be easily undone. Herodias experimented with new perfumes and did not speak of what she must have known, that Rebekah was Thaddeus' daughter who had run away. Rebekah had become her favourite hairdresser and she apparently did not want to lose her.

Shavuot was the celebration of when Moses received the Ten Commandments from God on Mount Sinai. The commandments would be read along with the story of Ruth, sacrifices made and special meals prepared. Herod had taken a few officers and slaves with him and returned a week or so after the festival.

A few days after Herod's return to Machaerus, Masika came to Rebekah again. She knew that Rebekah felt a deep sadness for Yehoshua and there was amazement in her eyes as she told her what she had learned in the early hours from Esau, who she had been with the previous night. He had been to Jerusalem with Herod for Shavuot.

'There are men and women who say that Yehoshua rose up from the tomb he was placed in after three days,' she whispered. 'At Shavuot one morning at nine o'clock, many pilgrims from distant lands heard God speaking to them in their own language. A man called Peter stood up and said the prophet Joel foretold of this time when God would pour out his Spirit on all the people. They are saying that God knew that Yehoshua would be crucified but would give him the power to overcome death. More than 3,000 people said they had been wrong about him and were baptised into the name of this Yehoshua.'

Rebekah lay down on her straw mattress as usual that evening and wondered if what she had seen in Yehoshua's face was something more than bravery. She could not sleep and after three hours of restless shifting, prayed silently: 'Lord God Almighty, please have mercy on me for the agony I have placed on my mother, and teach me if this Yehoshua was more than a prophet. If he came to show us what you are like, then please show me. I will follow you in my heart.'

With that she fell asleep. The next day Masika asked her what she thought about the story she had told her, and without giving herself time to think, Rebekah replied, 'Yehoshua is the one our fathers have been waiting for, but cruel men cannot see it.'

As soon as Rebekah had said this, she knew Masika would tell Esau, as she no doubt wanted to keep in his good favour. Even so, something had changed for Rebekah; she was still frightened but now she had someone to share her fear with; whatever happened, God would walk with her, through darkness or in the light. Her faith had become real, perhaps for the first time. She carried on with her daily duties wondering what would happen, for she knew something would.

Meanwhile, Herodias had sent Salome on a visit to Herod's great-nephew, Herod Agrippa, and upon her return she had some pressing news. One day after his return from Jerusalem, Herod was on the roof of the palace drinking wine in the late afternoon sunshine and Herodias came up and lay down beside him. Herod sensed she had something to say and waited. Herodias explained that Salome had been to see his great-nephew and it had become apparent that he was fully aware of the arms hoarding being undertaken in preparation for Herod's campaign to regain control over much of his father's former territory.

What Salome had also discovered was that Herod Agrippa was himself ambitious; and that ambition was more important to him than family loyalty. Herod would have to watch carefully because it was not simply the orthodox Jews and Pilate he needed to manoeuvre around. Herod thought for a while and suggested that Salome invite Agrippa to stay with them more often. Herod would seek to collaborate with his great-nephew, who perhaps would prove naïve when it came to understanding the treachery Herod was capable of.

Herod, pleased with himself for thinking up such a ruse, then changed the subject. 'One of my officers has told me that your favourite hairdresser has become a secret disciple of this Yehoshua, who some are saying has risen from the dead after being crucified by Pilate. Will she start to speak like Yohanan? After all, you do come from a priestly heritage and she may think that our marriage is invalid. And once she starts to think it, then what?'

Herodias did not want to lose Rebekah, but neither did she want a hairdresser who could cause trouble in the household by questioning her sexual habits and marriage to Herod. They argued over what to do. Rebekah could mysteriously vanish, but then, her father was a Pharisee who had visited Herod recently. He had not asked about his daughter, even though he was aware she was a slave in the royal household: he surely would not want anything to happen to her without the proper religious process being carried out. If Herod hadn't been told that she was Thaddeus' daughter he could have quite easily arranged for her to vanish, but now the situation was more complex. Having someone killed was not the issue; the problem was, who should do the killing? Neither Gideon nor Thaddeus had asked for Rebekah to be returned in order to administer punishment under their system, so Herod could hardly do so on their behalf, in case they preferred her to remain as a slave for him. Nevertheless, Herod did not want a follower of Yehoshua in his court.

Herodias paused and nothing was said for a few moments. 'Do this for me,' she said, at last. 'Train up another hairdresser in the next two weeks and then return this girl to her father's house in Jerusalem. That will keep you out of trouble, Herod, for the tradition is for the father to be responsible for his daughter's punishment. You sent Yehoshua back to Pilate to keep in with the common people; now send Rebekah back to her father so you can keep in with the Jewish leaders.'

Rebekah knew things were about to change. Masika began to shadow her while she did Herodias' hair. Herodias said she wanted an extra hairdresser for her daughter, Salome, but Rebekah knew this was not true. Salome's liaisons were spread over a wide area and there was no shortage of hairdressers available to the gentry and noblemen she associated with. Rebekah had heard talk about some of Yehoshua's followers being hunted down by the Temple lictors and even killed. She began to fear that now she would definitely be beaten and left to die in the hills, or sold to a far-off tribe. She cried out to the God of Israel in her heart, for mercy.

Then, early one morning she was told by one of the guards to put on some sandals and go upstairs with him. There another guard joined them and they left the fortress for Jerusalem. Rebekah was told to walk behind them. After sheltering for a few hours that night, they reached Jerusalem the next evening and one of the guards told Rebekah to direct them to her father's house. She could not understand why she was being taken home and began to wonder if it was a trick, or if her father had summoned her home to exact his own punishment on her.

When Esther came to the front of the house, she almost collapsed in shock; her face changed colour and her eyes widened. Rebekah was trembling and shaking and could not speak. The guard asked Esther where Thaddeus was, and she said he was ill in bed.

The house smelt of illness and Rebekah found out later that her father had been suffering with dysentery. The guard insisted on giving Thaddeus a letter personally and went inside. He came downstairs and with the other guard, left to return to Machaerus.

'Oh, my daughter!' Esther and Rebekah embraced, and then they cried. Eli came to see what was happening, and when he saw Rebekah, he also began to cry, hugging his sister, as she kissed his head and wept.

At last, Esther went upstairs to see Thaddeus. He was asleep and the parchment letter had been left by his side. Esther came downstairs with the letter:

To Thaddeus, the father of Rebekah

I am returning this slave of mine, Rebekah, to you for the determination of her fate and punishment, as she is your daughter. She is a suspected follower of Yehoshua and cannot, therefore, remain in my court. This letter will be delivered to you by hand by one of my officers.

King Herod Antipas

The letter was sealed with the royal mark.

Rebekah felt the guilt she had caused by abandoning her mother and started to say, 'I have caused you agony, Mother...' But Esther interrupted her.

'Stop, we will talk later; now we must look after your father... he is very ill and I need your help to keep him cool, especially at night. He experiences very bad cramps and we must sit with him and pray quietly to comfort him.'

'Yes, Mother, I will but I must tell you why I did it...'

'I know why you did it; you have more courage than I ever did, but your father is not like Malachi; he would have given you a short and brutal life. Despite everything, your father understands forbearance, Malachi does not. Come, let us tend to him.' She turned to her daughter, her eyes bright with tears. 'God has answered my prayer; I never thought I would ever see you...'

They hugged again. They had never known tears flow so easily.

Chapter Twelve: Home

Thaddeus was very unwell for several weeks. Esther and Rebekah tended to him, and there were times when they thought he would die. In the streets there was a great deal of trouble, particularly around the Temple where the followers of Yehoshua often congregated and taught about him as the Saviour of all nations.

They hardly left the house, but Esther's friends would sometimes call by to see how Thaddeus was. Each time a visitor came, Esther would hasten Rebekah out of sight: they were terrified their house would be attacked if it became widely known that Rebekah was there. They knew that Gideon was a powerful influence in the Sanhedrin and he would be bound to cause trouble of one kind or another; his anger was volcanic.

By now Esther and Rebekah had had many talks and Esther knew more about Solomon and Jacob, how they had rescued Rebekah and how Jacob's father, Joel, had been murdered by the Zealots. Rebekah told her mother that she wanted Thaddeus, once he had recovered, to meet again with Solomon. It was clear to Esther that Rebekah had some kind of affection for Jacob, but she pretended not to know.

Thaddeus slowly recovered and Rebekah kept out of his way as much as possible, for fear of what he would say. She did not know what emotions she might trigger in him.

Esther, emboldened by all that had happened, talked to Thaddeus about him meeting Solomon again. From what she had learned from Rebekah, Esther was beginning to think that Solomon had a measure of wisdom worthy of his name.

One morning after Thaddeus had finished his prayers, she approached him.

'Gideon can help us no more, he can only make things worse. You are not like him because when all is said and done you want your worship to be genuine and in accordance with the Lord's compassion for his people.

Solomon saved our daughter from an almost certain early death. The Lord has allowed her to come home. This Solomon is a wise man who is loyal to the law but understands mercy. Please talk to him, for my sake.'

'Esther, I am worried, even though Rebekah is no longer betrothed to Malachi. Gideon will probably still use the situation to humiliate me; that will give him more status in the Sanhedrin. I am not sure if he is more interested in himself than in the correct application of the law. If Rebekah stays here, I will be expected to administer more punishment, or if she is sent somewhere else, I will be asked to demonstrate that it is a consequence of her disobedience. If I give consent for Rebekah to marry anyone, it will be seen as a capitulation and I will have to resign from the Sanhedrin and we would be harassed by the Temple lictors. I do not know what to do; it is an impossible situation. How will seeing Solomon solve any of that?'

Esther simply said, 'Unless you talk to him, you will not know.'

Thaddeus thought back to the last Sanhedrin meeting when he voted to find someone to betray the whereabouts of Yehoshua. He knew he had voted out of fear and privately felt ashamed of himself. He wondered if Solomon could tell him more about Yehoshua, and so he decided he would ask Solomon to visit him. He also knew Esther would be pleased.

The invitation was issued quickly, and a few hours later Solomon arrived and they started their conversation.

'Thank you for inviting me to speak to you, Rabbi Thaddeus,' said Solomon, seriously. 'I have had it on my conscience to explain my actions more fully to you. When my grandson, Jacob, and I came across your daughter in distress at the side of the road, we were on our way to Galilee to visit my son Laban. He has a farm there near Kadesh., My other son, Joel, who also worked on the farm with Jacob, had been murdered by the Zealots because he had been seen talking to some Roman soldiers.

Jacob had come to live with me after his father was killed, and we were going back to visit Laban.

'We could either leave her where she was, or take pity on her. The scripture asking us to "be open-handed" towards the "poor and needy" in our land[23] came to me. I believed your daughter when she said that should she go back, you could be made to resign from the Sanhedrin. So we took her with us on the journey, as a slave. On arriving at Laban's farm, I was unable to make a judgement as to whether returning her immediately to you would result in her demise or not. I am sorry to admit this, but I had no direct knowledge of you, although I had heard in the Temple that you are a member of the Sanhedrin.

'My son Laban would be protected if he had a Jewish girl slave to prepare food in the correct way, and the knowledge of this would keep the Zealots away who, according to the rumours, were watching my son Laban very closely. So Jacob and I left her there while we returned to Jerusalem, when I informed you of the situation.

'Soon after our leaving, we received a message from Laban that she had disappeared. We did not know whether she had been abducted or run away. That is the truth, rabbi, and if I have dishonoured our traditions or failed to judge correctly between mercy and discipline, then I must ask God to have mercy on me, and to instruct me how to make amends to you through additional sacrifices.'

Thaddeus felt his face soften, and he paused before replying. 'I understand, and I appreciate the deep thought and prayer you have devoted to the issue. However, I still have to deal with Rebekah in a way that the doctors of the law will approve of, and anything that suggests that I condone her disobedience will incur their wrath. What makes it worse is that she has been sent home by Herod Antipas for me to deal with, because she is a suspected follower of this Yehoshua, who so many are now saying has risen from the dead. What do you say about him?'

---

23. Deuteronomy 15:11.

Solomon looked steadily at Thaddeus, who sensed he was with a truly honest man.

'When Yehoshua was in Galilee near our farm, he went to Karn Hattin, near Capernaum, alongside the Sea of Galilee,' Solomon said. 'Jacob and I walked there to hear what he had to say, as his reputation had gone before him. Whether he has risen from the dead or not, I cannot say, but his message was a simple one and not out of line with our Scriptures. The Lord declared through the prophet Joel: "Rend your heart and not your garments. Return to the <sc>Lord</sc> your God, for he is gracious and compassionate, slow to anger and abounding in love, and he relents from sending calamity."[24]

'But this Yehoshua,' Solomon continued, 'was saying that the time has come for prophecy to be fulfilled. He said the chosen people must become messengers to all the nations. All his teachings mean that our way of life is being threatened. The scales have justice on one side and mercy on the other. I fear that some of our teachers have replaced justice with punishment, and Yehoshua's voice has upset them. If the Temple lictors, who are desperately searching for his body, find him, then we will know he has not risen from the dead, but all the time they cannot, his followers will multiply... and some of them will be killed. If we had treated Yehoshua with mercy, then his followers would be following us as well. We should have spoken to them with compassion, and not stripped them and stoned them.'

Thaddeus could not work out exactly what Solomon thought of Yehoshua, but the effect of his description was making Thaddeus examine his own heart. He was thinking how to respond when Solomon brought the meeting to a close.

'Rabbi Thaddeus, thank you so much for seeing me, and before I go, I should tell you something that you should know. My grandson, Jacob, I believe, is fond of your daughter. I say that not because anything

---

24. Joel 2:13.

improper has taken place, nor because of words that have been exchanged, but simply because I know Jacob. The one thing I have told Jacob is that she is not free to marry without your permission; I knew he was disappointed when I told him. We did not know you then, and it meant she could not marry anyone. Nevertheless, I have not come here with such intentions; I came as I feel I have an obligation to explain to you in detail what took place and to make any necessary amends. Whatever your decision as to how to deal with the situation, I am truly humbled that you have given me this chance to explain myself to you. I will pray for your family, as I am sure you will pray for ours.'

With that, Solomon left. When Esther came in to speak to him, Thaddeus said nothing and Esther knew she best not question him.

Later on, he said to her that Solomon was a good man and was not to blame for what had happened. The next day, when Esther told Rebekah that her father had said that Solomon was a good man, her face gently brightened.

Thaddeus was perplexed and uncertain but as he had recovered from his illness, he would now be expected to attend the next Sanhedrin meeting. He suspected that it was known that Rebekah had been sent home. Herod Antipas wanted to distance himself from the problem, and the guards who had brought Rebekah back were unlikely to have been sworn to secrecy. Thaddeus anticipated that Rebekah's return was already known about, most probably through the grapevine which he knew, from experience, included many in the Sanhedrin. He was in no doubt that Gideon would use the situation, if he could, to bolster his stature as a guardian of the law.

So, Thaddeus finally took the risk; he dared to let his heart and mind touch the tinderbox of doubt. He was steeped in the Jewish Pharisaical tradition. The Torah was his guiding light and he had been brought up to believe there was only *one* correct interpretation of the law. Rebekah's disobedience had somehow made him question the very foundations of his understanding. In past times such questioning would have been dubbed as 'rebellion in the eyes of God' by other Pharisees. He felt unable to fall back on that any longer; instead, he now he found himself uncertain as to what God wanted him to do.

For the past few years, he had sought to emulate the likes of Gideon. He had now met someone equally as devout but with a humility that he would previously have counted as weakness; that person was Solomon. How had he found the balance between mercy and faithfulness? How had he been able to be honest without forcing his hand over his grandson, Jacob? Was there something in this that he should have brought to his relationship with Rebekah? Solomon had seen that justice and punishment were not the same. He realised that the teachers of the law should represent God's character as far as they could; that meant they should spend more time looking into their own hearts than determining the motives of others. Solomon had done just that, and Thaddeus had felt something change inside him after meeting him. Thaddeus wanted something of that kind of faithfulness.

When Solomon returned home, he sat quietly. His own battle was not between mercy and retribution; it was between grief and hope. For a long time he had worshipped the God of compassion, but the loss of his son had led him into an inner emptiness that he yearned to be free of. Before Joel was murdered, Solomon could still genuinely echo the psalmist:

> The LORD is gracious and righteous;
> our God is full of compassion.
> The LORD protects the unwary;
> when I was brought low, he saved me.[25]

---

25. Psalm 116:5-6.

But now his eyes were drawn to the verses immediately before:

The cords of death entangled me,
the anguish of the grave came over me;
I was overcome by distress and sorrow.
Then I called on the name of the LORD:
'LORD, save me!'[26]

In his life, Solomon had suffered the loss of his parents to Herod the Great, who sought to repress orthodox Jews, many of whom objected to his flouting of the ritual aspects of the law. Herod's police had dragged Solomon's parents off, and they had died in prison. Solomon then lost his wife to a violent fever when Laban was twelve and Joel ten, and now Joel had been murdered by other Jews. Solomon did not blame God for these tragedies; he blamed Herod and the Zealots for his parents' and Joel's death. He put his wife's death down to Adam's sin and the subsequent brokenness of creation. In his heart he struggled to bear all of this, and he wondered how much more he could cope with.

In spite of it all, Solomon wanted to remain faithful to God in his heart. He often thought of the story of Shadrach, Meshach and Abednego, Daniel's chosen administrators in the far-off province of Babylon. They refused to bow down to King Nebuchadnezzar's golden image and were thrown into a fiery furnace. They proudly said that their God could rescue them, but even if he chose not to, they would not bow down to a different god.[27] Solomon trusted God to walk with him through the fiery furnace of life and whatever might befall him, he would not renounce his God in favour of religious privilege. He had seen too many of his fellow rabbis do just that; even Herod the Great had died in a tormented

---

26. Psalm 116:3-4.
27. See Daniel 3.

state of mind after becoming intoxicated with his own murderous power over his family and his people. Solomon wanted to leave this world at peace with his God, even if he left it stricken with grief.

Chapter Thirteen: Resignation and Promotion

One day before the Sanhedrin was due to meet, Thaddeus decided to go to the Temple to pray. As he approached the Beautiful Gate which led up the stairs through the other courts to the male priestly court, he bumped into Gideon.

'Ah, Thaddeus,' Gideon said. 'No doubt you have encountered the followers of Yehoshua at the entrance to the Temple. Is your daughter with them, I wonder?'

'She is not,' Thaddeus retorted in defence. 'I will deal with her as I see fit, thank you, Gideon.'

'You can hardly blame me for doubting if you are up to the task, Thaddeus. Rebekah may have been punished, but has she shown any sign of repentance?' Gideon began to walk away, but called over his shoulder, 'The meeting tomorrow will focus on how we should deal with these disciples of Yehoshua, and your daughter will be no exception.'

As Thaddeus climbed the stairs, he felt the weight of Gideon's antipathy towards him and his family. He thought back to his conversation with Solomon; was he any less devout than Gideon? They did not differ in zeal, but Solomon's faith was a more selfless one; it seemed as if Solomon was equally loyal to the law, but did not appear to consider himself to be above it. Gideon never spoke about his own vulnerabilities before the Lord. King David in the psalms did the very opposite. Gideon's faith was very strong, but so was his opinion of himself; Thaddeus had at last begun to see through him.

It was difficult to find a place to sit in the Sanhedrin meeting the next day; the semicircle of seats was packed, with those who were late squeezing into the smallest of gaps. There were many young Pharisees present, eager to find out what was going to be done about Yehoshua's followers. The high priest signalled for quiet and asked what progress had been made in finding Yehoshua's body.

'We have searched high and low,' the head lictor replied, 'including the houses of those who most closely followed him, and we have found nothing. We will keep searching, but if the Sanhedrin wants us to now drive Yehoshua's disciples from Jerusalem, we will have to focus our energies on that mission. The stoning of his followers like Stephen will not be the last; it will be the only way to suppress the movement.

Thaddeus thought about this. Stephen, a follower of Yehoshua, had accused the Jewish leaders of persecuting God's chosen 'Righteous One, Yehoshua'. Stephen ignited their anger by asking them if there was ever a prophet their fathers had not persecuted, and his stoning was justified by the Sanhedrin as the appropriate punishment for blasphemy.[28] One phrase that rang out in the meeting was: 'They are lovers of peace but haters of the law!'

Throughout the meeting Gideon glanced across the circle of seats where the members sat, catching Thaddeus' eye from time to time. Thaddeus remained impassive. Then a young Pharisee named Saul suddenly caught everyone's attention. He started to address the whole court.

'In the Scriptures the Lord said to David, his anointed one, 'Go, for I will surely deliver the Philistines into your hands.'[29] Now the Lord is saying the very same to us about the followers of Yehoshua. Supply us with more guards to assist in the destruction of this evil sect. The Lord's people have a history of persecution. We are not the persecutors; we are the persecuted. Now it is time to avenge the flawed attack on our traditions which this Yehoshua has brought upon us.'

Funds were allocated to pay for more lictors to disperse, imprison and even kill the disciples of Yehoshua. The shouting and anger grew

---

28. See Acts 6:8 – 7:60.

29. 2 Samuel 5:19.

into a cacophony of accusations; no one was silent and such calls as 'death to the followers of Yehoshua' and 'let us rid this holy city of this deadly disease' abounded. Such was the fervour that the formal process of approval was forgotten. Thaddeus quietly slipped out before Gideon had a chance to corner him.

When he got home, he went to his room and spent a few hours on his own without saying anything to Esther. The next day he sent one of the servants out with a message for Solomon to come and visit him. Solomon came and after they had talked for an hour, he left.

It came as a complete shock to Rebekah; she was woken at two in the morning by Esther. She whispered to Rebekah that Thaddeus, Eli and Esther herself were leaving for Bethany, where Esther's brother lived. They would join Rebekah later. Rebekah was to keep silent and go with those outside who were waiting for her. Two men who looked like farmers took Rebekah to a place outside of Jerusalem, where they met Solomon and Jacob. Seeing Jacob, Rebekah felt her heart leap with joy, but this was no time for happy greetings. He gave her the briefest of smiles, but she dared to believe he was pleased to see her again.

They walked almost without a word through the night and all of the next day, arriving late at Laban's farm. Rebekah was exhausted but thrilled beyond measure; she could not believe she had made the journey once again, but this time with her father's approval.

A week later, a letter was delivered to the president of the Sanhedrin:

To our Revered *Nasi*, Rabban Shimon ben Gamliel

I am writing to tender my resignation from the Sanhedrin.

As you know, my daughter, Rebekah, absconded and was flogged and then sold into slavery by Malachi, son of Gideon, as a punishment for her disobedience to me. It has been announced that Malachi is no longer officially betrothed to my daughter and therefore the matter is closed. The following are my reasons for resignation.

I, of course, am concerned that the strict traditions of the elders are under threat by the recent growth of Yehoshua's followers. Without passing judgement in any way on the substance of Yehoshua's teachings, we are told in our own Scriptures that our Lord God is 'compassionate', 'gracious', 'slow to anger' and 'abounding in love and faithfulness'. This is repeated in Numbers 14:18, Exodus 34:6, Joel 2:13, Psalm 145:8, Psalm 103:8, Jonah 4:2, Nehemiah 9:17 and Exodus 34:6-7. Where there is judgement to be exercised, it is the Lord himself who visits the people up to the 'third and fourth generation'. So, I do not support the persecution and killing of Yehoshua's followers, regardless of whether they are right or wrong. I regret voting to capture with a view to killing Yehoshua at a previous meeting.

Secondly, the following is from the prophet Isaiah, chapter 53:

Who has believed our message
and to whom has the arm of the LORD been revealed?
He grew up before him like a tender shoot,
and like a root out of dry ground.
He had no beauty or majesty to attract us to him,
nothing in his appearance that we should desire him.
He was despised and rejected by mankind,
a man of suffering, and familiar with pain.
Like one from whom people hide their faces
he was despised, and we held him in low esteem.
Surely he took up our pain
and bore our suffering,
yet we considered him punished by God,

stricken by him, and afflicted.
But he was pierced for our transgressions,
he was crushed for our iniquities;
the punishment that brought us peace was on him,
and by his wounds we are healed.
We all, like sheep, have gone astray,
each of us has turned to our own way;
and the LORD has laid on him
the iniquity of us all.

He was oppressed and afflicted,
yet he did not open his mouth;
he was led like a lamb to the slaughter,
and as a sheep before its shearers is silent,
so he did not open his mouth.
By oppression and judgment he was taken away.
Yet who of his generation protested?
For he was cut off from the land of the living;
for the transgression of my people he was punished.
He was assigned a grave with the wicked,
and with the rich in his death,
though he had done no violence,
nor was any deceit in his mouth.

Yet it was theLORD's will to crush him and cause him to suffer,
and though the LORD makes his life an offering for sin,
he will see his offspring and prolong his days,
and the will of the LORD will prosper in his hand.
After he has suffered,
he will see the light of life and be satisfied;
by his knowledge my righteous servant will justify many,

and he will bear their iniquities.
Therefore I will give him a portion among the great,
and he will divide the spoils with the strong,
because he poured out his life unto death,
and was numbered with the transgressors.
For he bore the sin of many,
and made intercession for the transgressors.

My question is this: When the 'Righteous One' does come, how will we recognise him? At a recent meeting of the Sanhedrin, Rabbi Nathaniel said this: 'When the Messiah comes, he will come into this land as a child of one of *our* families, a family God will choose from *us*.' But the scripture says:

Like one from whom people hide their faces
he was despised, and we held him in low esteem.

How then does this scripture fit into Rabbi Nathaniel's claim? Either Rabbi Nathaniel is right or the scripture is right, but not both. I hope it is clear as to why I am resigning from the Sanhedrin with immediate effect.

I wish you every blessing of the Lord in these difficult times
Rabbi Thaddeus

On receipt of the letter Revered *Nasi,* Rabban Shimon ben Gamliel, immediately asked Gideon to come to see him. He showed Gideon the letter. Gideon paused before responding.

'We Sadducees do not believe in the resurrection; we believe solely in the Torah as God has given it to us through Moses. The Pharisees are very fond of quoting the prophets and using them to overturn the detail of the law. So Yehoshua's followers are deluded if they believe he has been raised from the dead. They are a threat to our faith, our land and our destiny. They must be crushed. As for Thaddeus, we are better off without him and his family. I have wasted too much time on him already. I should have known it was a mistake for Malachi to marry into a Pharisee's family; now I have found a family from our own, where the women know their place, their duty and their obligations. I think you should accept Rabbi Thaddeus's resignation with immediate effect.'

The *Nasi* nodded his assent and Gideon thanked him. It looked as if he was leaving but he suddenly turned and sat down again.

The *Nasi* looked at him expectantly. 'There is more?'

When Gideon spoke again, his voice was low, full of concern, and not a little hesitant.

'Yes. One further matter, *Nasi*; given your health and the tense times we are living in, would you consider me stepping into your shoes at least on a temporary basis until the next election of president? I will honour your approach and consult with you, but perhaps it would take the pressure off you till at least we have dealt with the followers of Yehoshua?'

The *Nasi* thought it through for a moment. 'You are the right person for this time.' He nodded. 'We will propose it at the next meeting.'

Gideon bowed his head in respect, rose and left, with a smile.

Chapter Fourteen: A Game of Stones

The following September, Jacob and Rebekah married in the glow of autumn in Galilee. The wedding was at Karn Hattin, near Capernaum alongside the Sea of Galilee, just near to where Yehoshua had taught about mercy and peace. Thaddeus, Esther and Eli attended, along with some uncles and aunts with their children. Laban, Solomon and many of the local farmers also joined in, while others stayed behind to tend all the sheep and other animals. Under the canopy, in the deep warmth of the sunshine, they celebrated; the wedding was traditional with the men and women staying apart until the day itself but afterwards everyone ate, sang and danced into the twilight.

By now, Jacob and Rebekah were both firm believers in Yehoshua, but they also sought to respect the traditions and the love shown to them by their families.

Thaddeus had given his consent for the marriage when he had last met Solomon in Jerusalem. Rebekah's parents and Eli had not returned to Jerusalem but now lived in Bethsaida on the edge of the Sea of Galilee, not far away from Laban's farm. Thaddeus ran a money-lending business and Esther did some embroidery which she sold at the local market. Jacob and Rebekah worked on the farm with Laban; Rebekah prepared the food in the traditional fashion.

In the months before the wedding, Rebekah had spent many hours talking with Jacob, asking him what he had felt when he had arrived back at the farm to find her gone. She told him she had thought about him a great deal when she was a slave. Jacob said his heart had plummeted when Laban told him she had vanished. Initially he thought Rebekah might have run off in fear. At that moment the strange longings he had felt towards Rebekah changed into a passionate need to find out where she was. Eventually, he went back to visit Solomon and discovered what had happened. By now Solomon had heard what had been discussed at the Sanhedrin, and knew that Rebekah had been kidnapped before being sold into slavery.

Jacob also told Rebekah what he knew from Solomon, that even if she were somehow to be freed, he would not be able to marry her without her father's permission. He had resigned himself that he would never see her again and tried to get her out of his mind.

'But I could not,' he admitted, and Rebekah had laughed.

'You knew you loved me that night when I delivered the goat's kid,' she told him, playfully.

'*You* delivered it! Didn't *I* have something to do with it?'

She laughed again, and this time, he joined in.

When Rebekah discovered what Thaddeus had written to the Sanhedrin, her love for her father rekindled and flowed into the love which she had always felt for her mother. Rebekah felt that her father's bravery had opened the door for their family's love to flourish naturally; joining their family to Solomon's was a natural extension. Rebekah wondered if her father could now see why she was a follower of Yehoshua and suspected that Solomon had always kept in his heart the thought that Yehoshua might be the Messiah.

The troubles were not over: Judea, Galilee and Samaria were torn apart with the anger of the Pharisees and the doctors of the law and their henchmen. They could not stamp out the new-found hope in the risen Yehoshua; the more they tried, the more the numbers following Yehoshua seemed to grow. The young Pharisee Saul who addressed the Sanhedrin with such venom had now experienced a miraculous conversion and began to talk to many people outside of the Jewish faith about Yehoshua; he was as fearless as he was previously murderous.

After the wedding, the family and friends stayed for a week. One evening, Solomon and Thaddeus were talking.

'Our fellow priests in Jerusalem are hoping that the Lord God will bring the Messiah through their offspring,' said Thaddeus.

'Our Lord God works in ways we cannot predict or understand,' replied Solomon. 'King David's line included Ruth, the Moabite, and our first great Temple was built by Solomon, my namesake. He was Bathsheba's second child – Bathsheba, the woman whose husband David had killed, the woman he then married. If through this mayhem the Messiah is to come, how then can we say that Yehoshua is definitely not God's "bruised reed"[30] sent to us?'

Thaddeus smiled as he answered. 'We cannot judge; sacrifice and burnt offerings are only there to change our hearts. Something changed my heart when I saw the murderous cruelty in the eyes of our leaders in the Sanhedrin. I knew that the Lord God was telling me to turn away. You have helped me make that turn, Solomon, and for that I give thanks to God with all my heart.' Thaddeus quietly recited some words from the prophet Isaiah which he had put in his letter of resignation to the Sanhedrin:

Yet it was the LORD's will to crush him and cause him to suffer,
and though the LORD makes his life an offering for sin,
he will see his offspring and prolong his days,
and the will of the LORD will prosper in his hand.

Jacob sat silently with the men as Rebekah rested her head on her mother's shoulder. The heat of the day lingered as the sun drifted down behind the hills. The smell of the food and wine along with the sounds of gentle conversation seemed very far off from the dank emptiness of Herod's slave quarters. Rebekah had not forgotten, and cast her mind back there for a moment in disbelief; she wondered how she now found herself by the Sea of Galilee marrying Jacob. She felt truly thankful to a God who had understood her own and her mother's suffering. She had seen Yehoshua taunted by Herod and the Pharisees with her very own

---

30. Isaiah 42:3.

eyes, but Yehoshua's face had had no fear in it; she was now beginning to understand why.

Although it was late, Eli came up to Rebekah.

'Play a game of stones with me.'

'All right.'

They picked up stones and Eli checked them to make sure they were all the right size. The game began.